"You called me *Savage!*"

Griff's words were harsh as he got up from the rumpled bed.

Watching him, Melinda stood, straightening her clothes. "Okay, so I called you Savage. What's the big deal?"

"How many times do I have to tell you," he asked furiously, "that the boy you knew as Savage is gone? He no longer exists."

"Then who the hell was making love to me just now?" Melinda asked, pointing at the bed between them. "I'm starting to think you're crazy."

"*I'm* crazy?" he said, throwing both hands in the air. "What was it you said when I kissed you? You wanted me wild and reckless and . . . uh . . ."

"Dangerous," Melinda supplied irritably.

"Well, I'm none of these things, Melinda. So, why don't you quit hanging on to the past?"

"Because you liked yourself, then—and I liked you," she murmured sadly.

"What would it take for you to like me again?" he asked, walking around the bed toward her.

"A leather jacket, perhaps. Maybe an earring or two . . ."

Ever since the publication of *Cause for Celebration*, **Gina Wilkins** has received many requests from her readers to write the story of Savage and Melinda. She says she toyed with several different plot ideas and tried to match the two characters with different partners. But they wouldn't let her do it.... Gina finally listened to Melinda and Savage and wrote their love story the way they wanted it to be told. The result is the deliciously provocative *A Rebel at Heart*. Enjoy!

Books by Gina Wilkins

HARLEQUIN TEMPTATION

174—HERO IN DISGUISE
198—HERO FOR THE ASKING
204—HERO BY NATURE
212—CAUSE FOR CELEBRATION
245—A BRIGHT IDEA
262—A STROKE OF GENIUS
283—COULD IT BE MAGIC
299—CHANGING THE RULES
309—AFTER HOURS

A Rebel at Heart

GINA WILKINS

Harlequin Books

TORONTO • NEW YORK • LONDON
AMSTERDAM • PARIS • SYDNEY • HAMBURG
STOCKHOLM • ATHENS • TOKYO • MILAN

To Valerie Hayward,
a wonderful editor and a good friend,
Savage and I both thank you
for liking him

Published March 1991

ISBN 0-373-25437-7

A REBEL AT HEART

Prologue

THE OCCASIONAL COUGH or cleared throat, a shuffle of clothing as bodies shifted restlessly in padded chairs, a pencil drumming lightly, rhythmically against the glossy surface of the cherry conference table— Griff found himself paying more attention to those secondary noises than to the report being monotonously recited by one of the other legal associates. Ten well-educated men of above-average intelligence surrounded him, Griff mused idly, and yet the earnest, overeager Mr. Feinfeld thought it necessary to read aloud a report that lay in front of each of them, neatly typed.

The pencil's tapping grew louder. Griff glanced to his left, to the end of the table where Wallace Dyson, the senior partner, stared fiercely at Mr. Feinfeld from beneath wavy gray brows. Mr. Dyson's gray wool suit, worn with a crisp white shirt and dark red tie, fit his health-club-toned body to perfection. Raising his hand to the uncomfortably tight knot of his similar dark red tie, Griff glanced from his own tailored gray suit to the other six gray suits in the room. They looked as if they'd been run through a photocopier, he thought, almost immediately suppressing his amusement.

He reminded himself that he fit in quite well with this respectably conservative gathering of men. No woman had, as yet, penetrated the upper management of this august legal firm in St. Louis, Missouri. After so many years of not fitting in anywhere, Griff was quietly satisfied to be one of the gray-suited clones in this legal conference room. He reached for the cup of lukewarm coffee in front of him and took a large swallow to wash down the sudden bitter taste in his mouth.

"If Mr. Feinfeld has nothing *original* to add to the financial report," Dyson said crisply when Feinfeld, who flushed at the stressed word, had finished speaking, "perhaps Mr. Myers would be gracious enough to give us an update on the Handel case."

The old tyrant was a stickler for formality. Griff's mouth twitched with a smile he wouldn't have dreamed of releasing as he turned his attention to Mr. Myers. The latter looked utterly miserable as he stood to make his report. "We've reached a settlement on the case, sir." He continued quietly, outlining the terms of the settlement, nervously watching Dyson for a reaction to the negotiations, in which Griff had played a major role.

Dyson nodded, then turned his steely gaze to Griff. "Mr. Taylor, you did make sure the settlement agreement included a stipulation that there be no further publicity about the matter?"

Aware of Myers's glare of irritation at Griff's involuntary intrusion into the report, Griff nodded, casually straightening his stylish glasses on the bridge of his nose. "Yes, sir. The publicity will end immediately after the settlement is made." And their client, a major pharmaceutical firm, would not be held publicly accountable for three deaths from a bad batch of medicine. It never failed to amaze Griff what a discreetly distributed couple of million dollars could accomplish.

"Good." Dyson's voice held as much approval as he was capable of expressing. Having handpicked Griff for his firm two years earlier, Dyson had grown fond of the younger man in his way.

It had been two years of swallowing pride, opinions and emotions on Griff's part, but the long hours, hard work and self-sacrifices had begun to pay off. At only thirty, Griff was firmly established on the upwardly mobile path to success, and he intended to stay on that path, whatever it took. No one would ever again look at him as if he were trash. He would never again be suspected of every nearby crime simply because he had a troubled home and a bad reputation. Respectable men no longer forbade him to date their daughters or sisters, but sought him as an eligible mate for those daughters and sisters. He intended to keep it that way.

Though, like many of Griff's co-workers, Myers resented the younger man's meteoric rise in Dyson's esteem, the man prudently kept his disapproval hidden as he completed his report. "The papers will be signed tomorrow, sir."

Griff was next. His report did not please Mr. Dyson at all. Dyson's brows drew lower and lower until Griff irreverently wondered if they'd end up below the older attorney's eyes. "She absolutely refuses to settle," Griff continued, discussing the trial currently underway involving one of their most influential corporate clients. "And there is little doubt that the jury will award actual damages for medical expenses and so on. What we're trying to prevent is an exorbitant award for punitive damages. To be honest, it's not looking very promising. The jury seems extremely sympathetic to the plaintiff."

"Just as we expected," Dyson muttered. "A frail little blonde in a wheelchair gets to 'em every time. Dammit, why won't she take the settlement? It's a hell of a good offer."

"She doesn't really care about the money, sir, other than her expenses, which she knows she'll recoup either way. She wants punitive damages on principle. She seems to have the idea that DayCo has gotten away with too many cases of negligence over the years by a judicious use of money she considers to be ill-gained. She also believes that our law firm has been too successful at defending powerful corporations who can afford the best legal assistance to thrash their less affluent victims."

Dyson frowned even more heavily, his eyes suddenly intent on Griff's face, making Griff wonder just what had come through in his voice. "Her words or yours, Mr. Taylor?" Dyson asked a bit too smoothly.

"Hers, sir." Griff refused to admit, even privately, that he'd found himself respecting the courageous young plaintiff's spunk.

Seeming to relax, Dyson nodded. "So what's on the agenda for tomorrow? Who's their next witness?"

"The woman's psychologist—to testify on the mental trauma angle," Griff replied. "Rumor is that the psychologist is fully supporting Miss Hawlsey in her pursuit of the punitive judgment. Seems to think it will help her put the trauma behind her."

"What do we know about this psychologist?"

Griff looked questioningly toward Bradley Corman, the legal clerk who'd been assigned to answer that particular question. Even Griff hadn't heard the details of the investigation yet.

A bit flustered at the shifting of attention to himself, Corman stood, frantically shuffling papers. "She's young—mid twenties—but successful. Associated with the Counseling Center in River City. She's only been there three months, having replaced one of the three original partners in the clinic at that time. A bit of a rebel—uses some rather unconventional methods of treatment, always involved in controversial social issues."

Dyson groaned expressively, making everyone aware that he knew the type and had no use for it. "Go on."

"There's not much else to tell, sir. She's single, hasn't been involved in any personal scandals, seems well respected by her co-workers and patients, despite her eccentricities. It seems everyone expects that sort of thing from psychologists. She's originally from Springfield, studied at Southwest Missouri for a couple of years, then transferred to the University of Tennessee. Her name is James. M.A. James."

Griff's head whipped around from his secretly amused study of his employer's disgruntled expression. "M.A. James?" he repeated to Corman.

Corman nodded. "That's right. M.A. James."

"Melinda Alice," Griff murmured, his lips quirking into a faint smile.

Dyson dropped the pencil and looked hard at Griff. "Do you know this woman, Mr. Taylor?"

"Possibly," Griff answered carefully. "The age, initials and hometown are right. She could be a girl I knew some years ago, Melinda James."

"And were you on good terms with the girl?"

"Yes, sir. Very good terms. We dated for a time before I joined the Navy."

At that, Dyson's dark eyes turned wary. "Do you still have feelings for this girl?" he demanded tactlessly. It was obvious that he would be very displeased if the answer was yes.

"No, sir," Griff answered dutifully—and truthfully. Melinda had been only fourteen when he'd known her, he barely eighteen. She and her twin had been orphaned at nine, raised after that by their older brother and two older sisters, the eldest of whom had been named their legal guardian. Despite her brother's objections, Melinda had been Griff's best friend at a time when he'd been desperately in need of a friend. Though his memories of her were warm ones, he had no desire to revisit his past. The old wounds were still too painful, too potentially damaging to the new life he'd so carefully built for himself. "We were only friends."

Dyson smiled. The other men shifted apprehensively in their seats. Dyson's smiles were always unnerving. Even Griff found himself needing to swallow.

"Then you know her weaknesses," the senior partner mused. His jaw squared, his eyes narrowed, his voice hardened. "Use them, Taylor. I want to win this case."

Griff winced. "It's been a long time since I last saw Melinda, but she was never one to intimidate easily. This may not be as easy as you think." He could clearly remember the young girl defiantly refusing to concede to her older brother's demand that she stop dating Griff. Matt James had been a man used to having his own way. Yet he'd lost that particular argument to his youngest sister—repeatedly.

"Nonsense," Dyson pronounced flatly. "She's a flaky shrink, you're a damned good lawyer. Take her out, Taylor. Show her up as the kook she is, question her motives for making a name for herself by putting her poor, traumatized patient through this ordeal, find out how much she's being paid for her testimony. I want to win," he repeated.

This time Griff gave in to the urge to swallow. "Yes, sir." *I'm sorry, Melinda. But I've come too far to turn back now.*

Griff intended to win. Whatever it took.

1

EVEN AFTER TWELVE YEARS, he would have known her anywhere. Fair skin. Thick, strawberry-blond hair. And those eyes—those slightly uptilted emerald-green eyes with little imps of mischief lurking in them. He'd never completely forgotten them.

She'd been lovely at fourteen—daring, outrageous, charmingly temperamental. She was incredibly beautiful at twenty-six—poised, colorfully chic, self-confident, but still with that almost invisible streak of defiant individuality that made her Melinda. The same defiance that had made her befriend him when few others had had the nerve to try.

And he was under orders to crush her.

She handled herself very well during questioning by the plaintiff's attorney. But then, they were on the same side. Twelve years ago, Melinda and Griff had been on the same side—the two of them against nearly everyone else. But he couldn't think of that at the moment. He was on DayCo's side now. The side with the money. The side with the power. Exactly where he wanted to be.

Would she recognize him? He'd changed a lot more than she had. Bleached, shoulder-length hair had been cut to a sedate, young-executive style in his natural sable brown. The earrings were gone, leaving only tiny, nearly invisible holes in his lobes as testimony to his former nonconformity. He dressed quite conservatively now in dark, tailored suits, white silk shirts, old school ties, thin-rimmed glasses. Gone were the leather and ragged denim, the wild colors and semiobscene screen-printed T-shirts. Even the name had changed. He'd left his youthful nickname behind when he'd left Springfield, answering now to his middle name of Griffin. Melinda had never even known his middle name, as far as he remembered. No, she probably wouldn't know him. Why should she? The angry young man she'd known no longer existed.

And then it was his turn to do the questioning. There was an almost palpable air of anticipation in the courtroom when Griff stood, taking his time about approaching the stand. Despite his youth, Griff was one of the best-known attorneys in Missouri, rapidly making a name for himself even outside the state lines. He was tough. He had a flair for drama that went well with his solid good looks. He had a knack for negotiating settlements in most of his cases that made both sides believe they were getting what they wanted. And on those occasions when a settlement wasn't reached, when the cases went to court, he rarely lost.

Big corporations wanted those qualities on their side in these frequent, high-stakes personal-injury cases. Political parties looked for those traits in future candidates for public office. He made no effort to discourage the courtship of either.

Feeling the eyes upon him, comfortable in the limelight in a way he hadn't been at seventeen, he cleared his throat. "Miss James—it *is* miss, not doctor?"

Her emerald eyes narrowed in the first sign of annoyance. "I have a master's degree in counseling, not a Ph.D.," she agreed coolly. "I prefer Ms."

He looked her over very deliberately, drawing the jury's attention to her eccentrically fashionable clothing and hairstyle. "Of course." His tone was dry, only faintly disdainful, holding not the slightest trace of the relief he felt. She hadn't recognized him. "Ms. James, you testified that as a result of her fall from the balcony of the resort cottage owned by my client, your patient, Miss Hawlsey, has been haunted by nightmares and an abnormal fear of falling. Is that correct?"

"Yes, that's correct. The trauma—the sheer terror Nancy Hawlsey felt during that devastating fall has stayed with her ever since. She honestly believed she was going to die, and that kind of soul-wrenching fear leaves emotional scars that often take much longer to heal than the physical injuries."

"'Soul-wrenching fear,'" Griff repeated in a toneless murmur meant to emphasize the dramatic phrasing. "Miss Hawlsey did sustain physical injuries in her fall. Yet she's suing for more than compensation for her medical expenses. She wants an additional two million dollars in punitive damages, as well. I understand you've encouraged her to pursue this suit?"

"Yes, because she needs—"

"Just answer the question, Ms. James. Yes or no?"

Melinda's chin squared angrily. "Yes."

"You think my client should be monetarily punished for your patient's bad dreams?"

"I think—"

"Yes or no, Ms. James?" he repeated with weary patience.

"Yes." She all but spat the word at him.

Good. He was beginning to rattle her. The less confident she looked, the better his case. "And just how much are you being paid to treat Miss Hawlsey and to testify on her behalf, Ms. James?"

"I don't see what—"

"How much, Ms. James?"

"I work in a health clinic, Mr. Taylor, with sliding fees so that people with problems are not turned away for lack of money. However, the standard rate is sixty dollars an hour for those who can afford it or have adequate insurance coverage. I understand the going rate for attorneys is at least twice that, isn't it?"

He could, of course, point out that the question was irrelevant, that he was the one authorized to ask questions, not she. He decided to use her question against her instead. "That's true, of course." He glanced at the jury as if to emphasize that he would not deny what everyone already knew.

"Once this case is decided, one way or another, my client will have no further need of my services. Can you say the same, Ms. James? Will a judgment in her favor completely cure Ms. Hawlsey of the traumatic aftermath of her accident?"

Melinda answered warily. "No, of course not."

"She will continue to need treatment?"

"Yes, probably. Her nightmares are debilitating, her fears making her almost dysfunctional in everyday living. I hope that with—"

"When do you expect her to be cured?" Griff interrupted bluntly.

She lifted her hands in exasperation. "I can't give an exact date. Surely you don't—"

"You're the one who pointed out that I'm being paid for my services, Ms. James. My response is that my client knows in advance approximately how long he will need to employ me. There is a point at which I will no longer be needed, and that point is quite clear to each of us—my services end with the decision of this jury. Is it too much to expect that you can also give *your* client some indication of how long she'll be obligated to pay sixty dollars an hour for you to soothe her fears? Is there some magical formula for you to calculate the exact amount of time or number of therapy sessions needed to cure a posttraumatic neurosis?"

Melinda drew a deep breath, her fair cheeks stained with an angry flush. "May I answer in complete sentences, Mr. Taylor, or will you continue to interrupt me after every few words?" Her voice was icily furious. He had to fight a nostalgic smile. How many times had he heard her sound that way after a fight with her older brother?

He gestured for her to speak, the courtly nod of his head just short of mocking.

"The difference between our two clients, Mr. Taylor, is that yours will leave this courtroom, no matter what the jury's verdict, and go on with his life as usual. If he loses, he loses only money, and he has plenty of that. He can always raise the rates at his hotels or increase the rent in his apartment and office buildings or liquidate some of his stock in major corporations. Or he can cut back expenses by authorizing more of the shoddy maintenance work that led to Nancy Hawlsey's accident.

"Nancy, on the other hand, will spend most of her life in pain as a result of the injuries to her back. She is able to be on her feet only a few hours a day, after which time she is confined to a wheelchair. Every time she closes her eyes, she relives the horror of having a balcony literally dissolve beneath her feet, feels herself falling, certain she's going to die in a crumpled heap on the ground. She's twenty-four years old, and she has many years of pain and therapy, both physical and emotional, ahead of her. A generous judgment by this jury will, at least, save her the worry of paying her bills. And your client needs to know that when he considers cutting corners to increase his profits, he is affecting the lives of people who trusted him to follow safety standards prescribed by law. He should be punished for forgetting that in the first place."

Griff silently admitted that he may have made a tactical error in allowing Melinda to speak. It hadn't been a bad closing argument, actually. She'd have had a great career in law. He couldn't imagine why he was feeling so damned proud of her—as if he'd had something to do with turning her into the articulate, idealistic, strong-willed professional woman she appeared to be. Such feelings could get him into big trouble.

He pushed one hand into his pocket, his pose casual, apparently unmoved by her discourse. "Miss Hawlsey has always had a fear of heights, hasn't she, Ms. James?"

Melinda nodded suspiciously. "Yes, she has."

"So severe, in fact, that she has sought treatment for the neurosis in the past?"

"Well, yes, but she was getting better. She did, after all, step out on that balcony to enjoy the view from her cottage."

"But the fall in itself did not create her fear of heights. It was simply an unfortunate accident that strengthened the fear she already had, isn't that right?"

"The accident should not have happened. That balcony had been in precarious condition for some time, according to the witnesses that have already testified. Had your client spent the money necessary to—"

"Again I am forced to remind you that I have asked you a question, Ms. James. One that requires only a yes or no answer. Did Ms. Hawlsey's fear of heights exist prior to her fall or did it not?"

"It did."

"Thank you, Ms. James. I have no further questions." Griff returned to his seat and leafed through his notes as if the psychologist's testimony was already forgotten, hardly important enough to retain his attention. He didn't look up again until Melinda was out of the stand.

He made no attempt to delude himself about what he was feeling. Relief that she hadn't recognized him. Reluctance to unearth parts of his past that he'd buried years before. Regret that this reunion with his former friend had occurred in such a way. Grief at the loss of one special memory from his youth. Even if she found out who he really was, Melinda would never forgive him for belittling her this way.

I'm sorry, Melinda.

MELINDA THREW HER PURSE on the floor. Then, for good measure, she threw her briefcase across her tiny office. "Obnoxious, arrogant, unethical, mannerless pig."

A sneaker-clad foot had been dangling rhythmically over the back of the low, deep-cushioned sofa that, along with an upholstered armchair and a battered desk against the back wall, took up all the available floor space in the room. At Melinda's noisy entrance, the foot disappeared. A moment later, a grinning sandy head popped up. Crossing his arms on the back of the couch, Fred Waller, one of Melinda's associates, cocked his head and studied her curiously. "Things didn't go well in court?"

"What are you doing in my office again? It's not as if you don't have one of your own."

"My, my, we *are* in a bad mood, aren't we? Tell Dr. Waller all about it, dear."

Rounding the end of the couch and sidestepping the armchair, Melinda headed grimly for her desk. "The attorney for the defense made a fool out of me. He asked obnoxious questions and then refused to allow me to finish my sentences. *Yes or no, Ms. James?* He taunted me into crawling onto a soapbox, then all but laughed at the lecture I gave. He treated me like an inferior, money-grubbing quack with no credentials, no ethics and very little intelligence. Imagine *him* having the nerve to condescend to *me* when he makes his living defending heartless, predatory capitalists like Arthur Dayton!"

Fred winced sympathetically, pushing his overlong hair out of his eyes. "I've heard that Taylor guy is one tough bastard. I mean, he's Wallace Dyson's fair-haired boy, which tells us something right there. Rumor is that Dyson's even got plans to make Taylor his son-in-law."

Melinda frowned, picturing the attorney who'd grilled her so coldly. Her first impression of him had been that he was a very handsome man, despite the almost obsessive conservativism of his clothing. Tall, well-built, dark-haired, confident, he'd made her heart beat a bit faster when her eyes had first met his deep chocolate ones through the lenses of his brown-rimmed glasses. There'd been a pull of—recognition? Attraction?

But, no. She must have been imagining it. He'd turned on her immediately and mercilessly, his first words to her a derogatory observation that she did not have a doctorate in her field. "Jerk," she muttered.

"You're looking at me, but obviously thinking of him, so I won't take offense," Fred observed indulgently. He crossed one denim-covered knee over the other, leaning back with his arms draped across the back of the blue couch, his position stretching his yellow T-shirt with its annoyingly cheerful advice to stop worrying and be happy. "How bad was the damage?" he asked more seriously. "Does Nancy have a chance of winning her case?"

Melinda sighed, pushing a strand of strawberry-blond hair from her face. "I think she has a good chance of receiving compensation for her medical expenses, maybe a little extra to help her get by. Of course, her attorney's fees are astronomical, so it will take an awfully large settlement to insure that she'll be adequately provided for. As for the punitive aspect she's pursuing—well, I don't know. Taylor's good. Damned good."

"Yeah, well, he'd have to be or he wouldn't be working for Dyson and Associates," Fred pointed out again. "Taylor's going places, and every new win in court is another step up the ladder for the guy. He'll do anything he has to do to get to the top, according to the grapevine. Got an eye on a political career, I hear."

Melinda wasn't surprised by the extent of Fred's knowledge of gossip. Fred was an avid people watcher, consumed newspapers and local magazines the way some people popped pills, remembered everything he read and heard. He was well suited to his career as a therapist. Since moving to River City—a suburban town some fifteen miles out of St. Louis—three months before, Melinda had learned a great deal about the area from him. She had become involved in community affairs. She was already familiar with Dyson's name and reputation, of course. She detested everything his firm stood for, and she specifically hated its position as favorite defender of the rich and powerful.

Dyson had grown rich catering to the wealthy, and pictures of him and his wife and beautiful young daughter appeared often in the social pages of the local newspapers. Melinda had met his daughter a time or two at local charity fund-raisers—events Melinda attended as a result of an active social conscience and Leslie Dyson attended because it was expected of her to be involved with socially approved causes. So Dyson had Taylor in mind as a husband for his daughter, did he? Mentally placing the couple side by side, Melinda's frown deepened. For some reason, the match bothered her. True, Taylor was a jerk, but he seemed too intelligent, too dynamic for blandly pretty Leslie Dyson.

Not that she cared, of course, Melinda reminded herself quickly. Actually, it would serve the guy right to find himself looking into those empty blue eyes across his breakfast table every morning. "Does Griffin Taylor come from a family in Dyson's social circle?" she asked with an attempt at nonchalant curiosity. That would explain how the man had made such advances in Dyson's firm at such a young age.

Fred shook his head. "Nope. He's only been working for Dyson for a couple of years. No one knows much about the guy, actually. It's almost as if he appeared out of the blue—or out of Dyson's daydreams of suitable son-in-law candidates. I've heard that Taylor received most of his education in the Navy, but no one's ever mentioned where he came from prior to entering the service."

The Navy. Melinda's head lifted sharply. She caught her full lower lip between her teeth, speculating. "No, it couldn't be," she mused a moment later, shaking her head firmly. "Just because he was in the Navy doesn't mean—" She paused, then frowned, worrying a lock of hair between the fingers of her right hand. "He's the right age, and his name *is* Taylor, but it's Griffin, not Edward."

Fred was looking at her strangely. "I'm sure this makes sense to you, but you lost me some time ago, Melinda."

She blinked him into focus, her thoughts still whirling with possibilities. "It just never occurred to me until you mentioned the Navy. I mean, Taylor is a very common name."

"That's true," her associate agreed gravely. "Not quite as common as Smith or Jones, of course, but still common."

Ignoring his frivolous observation, Melinda released her hair and worried a nub of a pencil lying on the desk in front of her, staring at it as if it held the answers to her questions. "No, of course it couldn't be. But his eyes were brown—no, his hair was wrong. Oh, but he bleached it. Of course, twelve years *would* make a difference."

"Melinda!" Fred almost shouted, standing to lean on the desk with braced arms and staring directly into her startled eyes. "What the hell are you babbling about?"

Realizing what she'd been doing, Melinda smiled apologetically. "Sorry, Fred. It just occurred to me that it's possible that I know the guy—or used to know him a long time ago. It's not probable, but it is possible."

Fred sighed gustily and returned to his seat. "Thank you for explaining. I was about to call for a straitjacket. Even for you, that was pretty weird."

"Oh, thank you so much." She made a face at the man who'd been her friend from the moment they'd met five months earlier, when they'd started to discuss the possibility of her joining the staff of the Counseling Center after being introduced by mutual acquaintances.

He nodded courteously. "You're welcome. What makes you think you knew the obnoxious, arrogant, unethical, mannerless pig at some point in your questionable past?"

She rolled her eyes. "*My* past isn't questionable. You just told me *his* is."

"Melinda—" Fred growled impatiently.

Chuckling, she relented. "There was a guy I knew when I was a teenager—barely a teenager, I was only fourteen. He was my first boyfriend."

"Which is probably why you remember him out of the hordes who succeeded him," Fred murmured wickedly.

Loftily ignoring him, she went on, "His name was Edward Taylor, but he despised the name Edward and would answer only to the name of Savage. A true rebel. He wore dangling earrings and torn denim at a time when only the most avant-garde rock stars were doing so—certainly none of the nice boys in Springfield. He joined the Navy immediately after he graduated from high school. He promised to write, but I received only one letter and then I never heard from him again. He'd be thirty now."

"Well, the age is right, but the rest . . ." Fred looked doubtful.

"I know. It's just that there was a moment today when I thought he looked familiar, and when you said Navy—but he's probably not, of course."

"Now don't start jabbering again," Fred warned.

"I won't," she promised. "Besides, I don't even want it to be the same man. Savage was wonderful—a tough, belligerent bad boy with a caring, philosophical side that he allowed very few people to see. I was one of those people, perhaps the only one at the time. I adored him. I missed him horribly after he left, but I was young and I met other people, other interesting young men. I haven't really thought about him in a long time, but my memories of him are very special. I'd hate to think that bright, defiant rebel sold out for power and wealth."

"I can't picture Griffin Taylor as the young man you've just described," Fred admitted with a grin.

Melinda couldn't help smiling in return. "No, neither can I. It's just a coincidence, of course, that the last names and the ages are the same. That's all it could be."

Fred studied her a moment, then laughed ruefully and pushed himself off the couch. "You're not going to rest until you know for certain, are you, Melinda? I know you too well."

Startled, she stared at him. "What are you talking about? I have no intention of pursuing this any further. I don't care if I never see that creepy Griffin Taylor again—ever!"

"Now is that any way for a respected psychologist to talk?" Fred chided indulgently, heading for the door. "You're supposed to find something of value in everyone, remember?"

"Hmph." Her mutter expressed what she thought of that philosophy. Melinda never had been one to do as she was expected—in business or in her personal life. Her propensity for defiance had gotten her into trouble more than once.

"I'm cutting out of here. Bev and I have a date tonight. Just wanted to see how things went in court. Sorry it was such an ordeal for you."

Melinda shrugged. "I didn't expect it to be pleasant. I just hope I didn't blow things for Nancy."

"I'm sure you did just fine. Go home soon, all right? Get something to eat, take a nice, long bath, read something fluffy and escapist. Take your mind off it. There's nothing on your desk that can't wait until morning."

"I won't stay long," Melinda assured him, though she was already reaching for a stack of paperwork. "See you tomorrow, Fred. Tell Bev hi for me."

"Sure." He stepped out the door of her office, then poked his head in for one last comment. "Let me know when you find out whether this is the same Taylor, will you? You've got me curious."

"I told you, I'm not going to snoop into Griffin Taylor's background!" Melinda retorted, exasperated. "I don't want to know."

"Uh-huh. Right." Rolling his eyes in exaggerated disbelief, Fred left, whistling an off-key rendition of "My Boyfriend's Back." *Hey, na, hey, na.*

Mumbling disgruntledly, Melinda went to work. But even as she forced herself to concentrate on the paperwork in front of her, she wondered just what Griffin Taylor looked like without his glasses. She tried to picture him with longer hair, earrings and eyeliner. The image made her giggle.

"Leave it alone, Melinda," she told herself aloud. "You've got better things to think of. Much more important things."

She wondered what had happened to the angry young man who'd called himself Savage.

2

SHE HADN'T BEEN SURE he would see her, particularly without an appointment, but his secretary received permission for Melinda to enter Griffin Taylor's office. Actually, even his secretary seemed a bit surprised that Taylor had agreed to see his unexpected caller.

Taking a deep breath for courage, Melinda squared her shoulders, lifted her chin and opened the door to the office. She couldn't help comparing his office to her own, less elegant one. The carpet in hers was a bit worn, the arms of the couch and the one comfortable chair slightly frayed. Her cracked plaster walls were covered with inexpensive colorful prints. Her desk was battered and impossibly littered with files, papers, reference books and cassette tapes. Griffin Taylor's oak-paneled office was furnished in expensive antiques and had been decorated by a professional. She could have applied her makeup in the glossy reflection of his over-size desk, on which sat nothing but a walnut and gold desk pen set. This evidence of the profit he made defending his powerful clients brought her chin up even higher.

He stood politely when she entered the room, rounding the desk to offer her his hand. "Ms. James, this is a surprise," he remarked, his expression unreadable. "What can I do for you? Or did you drive all the way into St. Louis to gloat about the nice settlement the jury awarded your client?"

He was still gorgeous, dammit—even more so this close up. She tried to convince herself that she didn't care. And she wondered how he'd look when he smiled. If he ever smiled. Reminding herself of the purpose of her impulsive visit, she stiffened her spine. "I just wanted to tell you exactly what I thought of your behavior in that courtroom last week," she informed him. "As for gloating, we both know that your client intends to tie that money up in appeal courts for as long as possible and then—"

He did smile then, though rather grimly. "Believe me, Ms. James, there is nothing you can say about my courtroom manner that I haven't already heard many times. If that was all you wanted—"

"Don't dismiss me like that!" she snapped irritably. "Is it some kind of compulsion with you to interrupt people, Mr. Taylor? Does it give you a feeling of power?"

"Ah. You're here to analyze me." He leaned negligently against his desk, arms crossed at his waist, studying her coolly through his glasses. "Well, that's been attempted before, as well, Ms. James, so again, you're wasting your time." *And mine*, his tone implied.

Her fingers clenched into fists at her sides. "I'm not here to analyze you," she answered deliberately, trying to stay calm in the face of his goading. "I was in town anyway, and I stopped by only because there were a few things I wanted to say to you, and I knew I wouldn't be satisfied until I had said them, whether they make any difference to you or not."

"Oh, yes, the psychologist's favorite advice. Get it off your chest. Don't let the anger fester inside you." He made a sweeping gesture with his hand, implying indulgence. "Well, go ahead, Ms. James. Speak your piece. Then you can go, your unresolved anger relieved, your psyche restored to its usual good health. Far be it from me to cause you emotional stress."

"Ooh—" Fury made her almost speechless. She'd never been treated so condescendingly in her life—well, not since her bossy older brother had finally conceded that she was an adult and stopped telling her how to live her life. "Are you always this obnoxious, Mr. Taylor, or do you have something against psychologists in general?"

"I'm not particularly fond of the species as a whole, but I suppose obnoxiousness comes naturally to me," he replied with a hint of wry humor that surprised her. Then, as if he'd read the slight softening in her eyes, his faint smile vanished and his arrogant manner returned. "Spit it out, Ms. James. I have work to do."

Melinda eyed him suspiciously. Why did she suddenly suspect that he was deliberately trying to anger her for some reason? She pushed her hands into the deep pockets of her ankle-length fuchsia skirt, hoping the gesture would keep her from going for his throat. With exaggerated nonchalance, she began to wander around his office, casually studying the carefully placed accessories.

"If I *were* here to analyze you, Mr. Taylor, I would surmise that there is a reason you seem so compelled to fit the mold of successful, conservative young attorney. Something you're trying to hide, perhaps? A streak of recklessness that fights to get out, threatening the safe, comfortable niche you've carved for yourself?"

Sensing that he'd stiffened abruptly at her words, she congratulated herself on an astute guess. Without giving him time to respond, she pursued the slight advantage his discomfort had given her. "You know, a person can learn a lot by looking at a man's office. It's almost as revealing as his home. This painting, for example. Not much color, blandly chic. You didn't pick it out, I'm sure, but you've allowed it to remain. The gold pen on your desk. A gift to yourself in celebration of a personal victory? This little—"

Her words drifted off abruptly, her eyes freezing on the small, rectangular plaque sitting unobtrusively on one corner of his credenza. The three- by four-inch block of stained wood had been bordered with hand-painted, improbably shaped flowers, their colors just short of garish. Four crookedly lettered words were centered within the flower garland. *You've got a friend.*

The silence lasted a long time. Then Melinda clutched the plaque and turned to face him. He was as expressionless as ever, though his dark eyes had sharpened warily. He stood as if prepared for an assault. Why? she wondered hazily. What threat did she represent to him?

"You kept it," she said quietly.

He nodded. "Yes. It was the only thing I kept when I left."

"You weren't going to tell me who you are, were you?"

"No."

He hadn't even hesitated. She tried not to show how the curtly spoken word had hurt. "Why?"

He shrugged, turning partially away. "It wasn't relevant."

"Not—" She shook her head in slow disbelief. "We were friends."

"We were kids. It was a long time ago. We don't even know each other now. Besides, I had a job to do and you were in my way. I couldn't let old memories interfere with my effectiveness."

Her eyes closed in a moment of disillusion. Grief for shattered, sweet memories, memories that hadn't been allowed to interfere with his job. "What happened to you, Savage?" she whispered.

He whirled to her then, his eyes snapping, his jaw hard. "Don't call me that! The boy you knew no longer exists, Melinda. I put him away with all the other garbage from my past. I've made something of myself now. I'm not the bad boy from the wrong side of the tracks, the automatic suspect in every crime, the poor, disadvantaged kid whose mother left him with an abusive, alcoholic father. I've got respect now, and I earned it! No one needs to know about my past."

"You kept this," she said again, motioning with the little plaque she'd made him as a project for art class.

A muscle flexed in his jaw. "Yes. It was the only thing anyone ever made for me. It became a habit to keep it around—a good-luck token, I suppose."

Twelve years was a long time to hold onto a good-luck token. She didn't bother to point that out. It hurt too badly to know that he'd put his memories of her away with the uglier memories of his youth.

She took a moment to study him, comparing the hazy memories of the boy he'd been to the man who stood before her. He'd been almost thin then, his face softer. He was solid muscle now, and his face held all the softness of roughly hewn granite. She remembered the slight cleft in his chin. She'd once called it cute. She wouldn't use such an adjective to describe him now.

Only his eyes were the same, though their impact was lessened by the conservative glasses he'd adopted. They were still deep chocolate, framed in thick black lashes. He'd once emphasized that frame with eyeliner, she reminded herself in near disbelief. Only someone who was looking very closely could detect the banked anger, the ready temper that simmered in those dark depths. She wondered how many others in recent years had bothered to look beyond his bland facade to discover those lurking emotions in his eyes.

"I guess this means you don't want to have a drink to discuss old times and chuckle about the coincidence of ending up in the same city and the same courtroom." She tried to keep the words light, as if it mattered no more to her than to him.

He hesitated, then sighed, smoothing a hand over his crisply cut brown hair. "I'm sorry, Melinda. Sorry we had to meet again like this. Sorry for what I had to do in that courtroom. I wish . . ." He shook his head. "No. I can't think about the past now. I've taken great care to keep it buried and I can't risk having it come out now. It wouldn't be too hard for anyone to find out the details, of course, but so far no one's been curious enough to investigate. I'd like to keep it that way."

"In other words, I'm an uncomfortable reminder of your unhappy past, and because of that you want me to disappear. Is that correct, counselor?" Her tone was deliberately mimicking of the manner in which he'd interrogated her in that courtroom.

He sighed again, more deeply this time. "You always were one for blunt speaking. I see that hasn't changed."

"Yes or no, Mr. Taylor?" she asked coldly, the imitation still acridly intentional.

"Yes."

She kept her face perfectly still. "Fine. I'll get out of your office. Out of your life. You can forget we ever crossed paths again. Far be it from me to cause *you* emotional stress."

Setting the plaque exactly where she'd found it, she walked smoothly to the closed door, reached for the knob and turned it. Holding the door slightly ajar, she turned for one last shot. "By the way, I still haven't told you what I thought of your performance last week. I thought you were conceited, ill-mannered, insulting and offensive. Now I can add hypocritical to the list. Goodbye, Savage."

She made her escape, closing the door behind her before he could respond. Blinking away a film of tears, she passed his curious secretary and left the offices of Dyson and Associates behind her.

At twenty-six, she felt as if she'd just taken the final step away from the innocence of childhood.

"WHY ARE YOU SO SURPRISED, Melinda? No one stays the same forever. And twelve years is a long time."

Melinda made a face at her twin sister's calm practicality, which she would have done even if they hadn't been talking long distance over the telephone. "I know, Meaghan. And I wouldn't have expected him to be exactly the same, but I thought I would have at least still liked him."

"I don't know why," Meaghan replied frankly. "I never knew what you saw in him in the first place. He always scared me half to death. All that long, shaggy hair and earrings and eyeliner. All those fights he got into. I always knew he'd end up involved with the law, but I expected him to be on the wrong side of it."

"Actually, he's just your type now." Melinda was only half teasing. "Button-down collars, silk ties, conservative haircut. He's got Young Republican written all over him. He and John would probably be very good friends."

"Now don't start on John again," Meaghan warned in resignation. Her husband and her twin had waged a good-natured ideological war since they'd met four years earlier. Meaghan knew that Melinda genuinely liked John but couldn't imagine herself married to him or anyone like him. "And I still don't understand why you're so hurt by Savage's snub. It's not as if you've carried a torch for him or anything. The two of you were just friends. You weren't old enough for anything else. You said yourself that he only kissed you once."

"But it was my first kiss—from my first boyfriend," Melinda murmured nostalgically. "Does anyone ever really forget that?"

"Mm. And if he'd stayed around Springfield much longer, that wouldn't have been all he'd been first at. And our quick-tempered brother Matt would have killed him. With a little help from Grant and Tim," she added, naming their two older sisters' husbands.

"You make it sound like I was all set to fall right into bed with him," Melinda accused. "You know I waited a lot longer than most girls to take that particular step. We *both* did."

"Partially because of the way we were raised. But with you I always suspected it was because you compared every guy you met for years with Savage. Despite the impressive numbers of men you've dated, I know exactly how few you've allowed to get really close."

"You think I've compared every man I've dated to a boy I knew when I was fourteen?" Melinda repeated incredulously. "Come on, Meaghan!"

Meaghan made a hasty retraction. "Just a theory—I could be wrong. Maybe you've been looking for a man just like our beloved brother."

Melinda had to laugh at that one. Her battles with their admittedly autocratic brother had become family legends. "So who says I've been looking for anyone?"

"I do," Meaghan returned without hesitation. "You're the only one in the family who hasn't married, and you confessed last Christmas that you'd love to have children of your own eventually. You just haven't found anyone who suited you yet. Not for lack of applications, I might add."

"Oh, sure. I turn down at least two marriage proposals a day. Give me a break, Meaghan. I'm only twenty-six. Not exactly past my prime. And how did we get on this subject, anyway? All I was doing was telling you what a jerk Savage has turned into. He won't even acknowledge that he once went by that name, by the way. He's Griffin Taylor now—Griff to his friends. Isn't that a nice yuppie name?"

"I thought his name was something like Edgar or—"

"Edward," Melinda supplied. "He always despised it— I think because he was named after his father. I don't know where Griffin came from. Maybe it's his middle name. He never would tell me his middle name. Claimed he didn't like it any better than his first."

"Not that you remember him all that well," Meaghan teased. "When's his birthday?"

"May fifth. Want to make something of it?"

"Not I," her twin replied, laughing. "So you won't be seeing him again?"

"Not intentionally." Melinda's voice had turned grim.

"It really is a shame that things went so badly between you two," Meaghan sympathized, suddenly serious, as well. "I know how fond of him you were. It must have been very disappointing for you to find out that you no longer even like him."

"Yes, it was. But it's no big deal. I haven't seen him in twelve years. It won't change my life never to see him again."

Meaghan thoughtfully changed the subject, asking about Melinda's work. Melinda loved being a psychologist as much as Meaghan enjoyed her work in special education, two topics they could always talk about for hours. And then it was time to bring their weekly telephone call to an end.

"Kiss John and Andy for me," Melinda instructed, reluctant, as always, to break the connection.

"I will. Take care of yourself, honey. I miss you."

"I miss you, too." Only other twins could understand the bond between Melinda and Meaghan, despite their differences, despite the miles that separated them since Meaghan had married and moved to Tulsa and Melinda had accepted the job offer in River City. They were together every time they had the chance; being from a close family of siblings, the opportunities to see each other were frequent as someone was always planning a reunion for one occasion or another.

Sighing, Melinda stood and walked away from the telephone, heading for the small kitchen of her apartment in search of food. As she'd told Meaghan, she had no intention of setting eyes on Edward Griffin Taylor again. But she couldn't help thinking wistfully of a boy with angry brown eyes and an unexpectedly sweet smile, of the tender way he'd always spoken to her. *"Hey, yo, Melinda! Over here!"*

Laughing softly at the memory, she opened the door of her refrigerator, pleased that she was still able to treasure those moments from her past despite the disappointment of the present.

GRIFF STARED at the apartment door in front of him, hesitated, started to turn away, then swore beneath his breath and faced it again. Before he could change his mind, he lifted his hand and rapped firmly on the door.

Expecting to have to identify himself, he was rather surprised when the door opened almost immediately. Melinda was obviously shocked—and just as obviously not pleased—to see him. "What do *you* want?"

"I'm sorry," he said without preamble. "I was a jerk in my office yesterday. You caught me off guard and I reacted on instinct and I was wrong. There's no reason you and I can't still be friends."

"There's one," she replied evenly. "I don't like you any more." And she started to close the door in his face.

Griff caught it easily, exerting enough pressure to hold it open. "Let me in, Melinda. We need to talk."

"No. You've said all you needed to say. I'm an unfortunate reminder of the past. And you're so ashamed of that past you don't even want to remember the good parts. I was there for you when you were the one on the wrong side of the tracks, but now that you're the big-shot lawyer, you have no time for a mere psychologist from a health clinic. As I said, Mr. Taylor, you're a hypocrite, and you should remember that I've never had a use for hypocrites."

"No one's tamed that mouth of yours yet, I see."

It wasn't the wisest choice of words. He could almost see the sparks ignite in her narrowed green eyes. "No, Mr. Taylor, no one has *tamed* me, as you put it. No one but Matt has ever been stupid enough to try— and he conceded defeat a long time ago!" She tried again to slam the door.

Griff pushed a bit harder and slipped through before she could stop him.

She whirled to face him, hands on her slender hips, almost quivering with rage. He noted dispassionately that she still tended to dress in loud colors and outrageous styles, even after all these years. "Didn't you hear me? I want you out of my apartment. How dare you—"

"Melinda, please. Not the how-dare-you speech. Couldn't we just talk rationally?"

His weary interjection stopped her short. "I am being rational," she muttered, tugging irritably at the hem of her multicolored knit top.

"May I sit?" He didn't wait for her to reply before making himself comfortable on her overstuffed white couch. He made a leisurely survey of the room, attention lingering on various oddities with which she'd chosen to decorate—a pink porcelain flamingo, a wall grouping of china masks representing flappers and dappers from the twenties, a lamp shaped like a geisha girl holding a candle. "I like your apartment. It's rather eclectic, to say the least, but I wouldn't have expected anything else from you."

"Please make yourself at home." She made no effort to tone down the broad sarcasm.

"Why, thank you. I don't suppose you have any coffee made?"

"No, I don't." She plopped gracelessly into a blue-and-white-striped wing chair, curling her bare feet pointedly beneath her.

Getting the message that she wasn't going to be the gracious hostess, he shrugged. "I need to cut back on the caffeine anyway. So how's your family? What's Meaghan up to these days? And you mentioned Matt— is he still his same overbearing self?"

"Sav—" She stopped at the look he shot her and exhaled impatiently. "I can't help it," she answered his silent remonstration. "It's what I always called you. I don't know what to call you now."

"My middle name's Griffin. I use that now, as you know. Most people call me Griff."

"Griff," she repeated coolly. "Fine. I can't believe you showed up on my doorstep and started asking about my family as if you hadn't told me yesterday that you'd appreciate it if I'd get out of your office and your life and stop making a nuisance of myself."

"I apologized for that. You didn't used to be one to hold a grudge, Melinda."

"You're the one who pointed out that we really don't know each other any more." Her smile was deliberately saccharine. "I don't invite strangers into my home for chats, Griff. Especially strangers I don't like."

"Are you going to start that again?"

"Why shouldn't I? It's the truth."

He leaned forward, resting his forearms on his knees as he looked at her. "What would it take to make you like me again?"

She eyed his muted blue plaid shirt and neat gray poplin slacks. "A leather jacket, perhaps. Maybe an earring or two."

"Sorry, that I can't do. Are you saying that all your men friends wear leather jackets and earrings?"

"No," she admitted. "But they don't pretend to be someone they're not, either. My friends are real."

"I'm real, Melinda. This *is* the way I am now. Twelve years have made a difference in my life. I'm not the same person I was then."

"So you keep saying. And, since that other person was my friend, you and I have nothing further to say."

He chuckled ruefully and shook his head. "How is it that you haven't changed at all in twelve years? You're still the same hotheaded, fast-mouthed girl you—"

"Woman," she interrupted firmly, straightening abruptly in the chair. "I'm not a girl any more, Griff."

He made a leisurely survey from the top of her strawberry-blond head to her bare pink toes, noting the slender curves between. "Yes, I'm aware of that."

He had the satisfaction of seeing a faint blush stain her fair cheeks. "Stop that," she snapped. "We both know you're not interested in me that way, either."

"I'm not?"

"No. Everyone knows Wallace Dyson has picked you for a future mate for his daughter, Leslie. I'm quite sure you have no objections, since you're so all-fired set on becoming wealthy and respectable."

He leaned back and made himself comfortable, concealing the faint ripple of unease her words caused. "My, you have been listening to the gossip mongers, haven't you, Melinda?"

"Isn't it true?" she challenged him.

He shrugged. "I've been out with Leslie a time or two. Regardless of what Dyson's hopes may be, I will be responsible for all decisions concerning my future. At this time, I have no plans to marry."

"Spoken like a true future politician."

Letting that pass, he changed the subject. "Have dinner with me tonight."

"No."

"Why not?"

"I don't want to. Besides, I have another date."

He hadn't expected that answer. He didn't like it. "Someone special?"

Her eyes laughed at him. "They're all special."

Torn between walking out and shutting her beautiful smart mouth with a kiss, he glowered at her. "You know, I'm just beginning to realize that your brother may have been justified in threatening to turn you over his knee a few times when you were growing up."

"He only threatened. He never quite got around to trying it."

"Maybe it's time someone did." He kept his voice bland.

"The guy in the leather jacket and earrings may have had the nerve to try," she answered equally coolly. "The yuppie attorney wouldn't stand a chance in hell."

There had been a time when he couldn't turn down a challenge. He told himself he was long past that. "You're the one who suggested we have a drink for old time's sake. When? Tomorrow? Or have you lost your nerve?"

She laughed at that. "I'm the psychologist, remember? That strategy won't work on me."

"So you're backing out?"

"I'm not backing out," she began heatedly, then stopped and glared at him. "All right, dammit, tomorrow."

He pushed himself off the couch. "I'll pick you up at seven for dinner."

"I never said anything about dinner!" she protested, rising hastily to her feet. "I said a drink."

"Fine. We'll have a drink with dinner. Good night, Melinda."

He gave her little chance to respond, slipping out the door while she was still groping for an appropriately scathing answer. He wasn't sure why he'd asked her out, he mused as he climbed behind the wheel of his expensive sports car. Maybe it was still too hard for him to turn down a challenge. And maybe it was because it bothered him more than he wanted to admit that Melinda no longer liked him.

There'd been too many times lately when he hadn't particularly liked himself.

3

MELINDA SQUIRMED RESTLESSLY in her seat, peeking surreptitiously through her lashes at the man seated across from her. They'd been in the restaurant fifteen minutes and it had already become painfully clear that, despite their brief past history, she and Griffin Taylor were the strangers he'd declared them to be. Twelve years was a long time—particularly when those years spanned the transition from childhood to adulthood. Griff Taylor at thirty was dramatically different from eighteen-year-old Savage, just as Melinda was different at twenty-six than she'd been at fourteen. That gap loomed in front of her as she studied the attractive, sober man across the table.

She wondered if he'd worn the navy pin-striped suit and white-on-white shirt to remind her of exactly how different he was now. She wasn't sure whether she'd chosen one of her more unusual ensembles—a vintage mauve satin chemise—to demonstrate that her changes hadn't been as drastic. Griff's eyes had widened when he'd seen her in the slinky, revealing dress that she'd accented with long strands of heavy beads and numerous bracelets, but he'd made little comment other than an innocuous remark that she looked very nice.

He cleared his throat, then suddenly smiled. "I think this is what they call an awkward silence."

One thing hadn't changed, she reflected. His unexpectedly charming smile still made her stomach quiver. "I think you're right," she managed calmly enough.

Resting his forearms on the edge of the table, he made a visible effort to relax while they waited for their orders. "We have a lot of catching up to do. I'd like to hear about your family. How are they?"

"They're all fine. Things have changed a lot, of course, since you knew us. Everyone's married now."

His brow quirked upward in interest. "Even Meaghan?"

"Yes. She and John have an eight-month-old son."

He shook his head in wonder. "It's hard to imagine." His smile deepened. "Did she marry an honor student? Student body president?"

She laughed. "Exactly. President of the Young Republicans in college, Phi Beta Kappa, Outstanding Young American. He's in banking."

Chuckling, Griff toyed idly with the stem of his wineglass. "Some things don't change, I guess." He shot her a quizzical look. "And do you still date the men most likely to raise your brother's blood pressure?"

"I date men I like," she answered flatly, then moved the conversation on. "You remember my older sisters, Merry and Marsha, of course."

"Sure. Do they still run their theme-party service in Springfield?"

"Yes. They've branched into catering, too. Very successful. Their husbands, Grant and Tim, are partners in a computer consulting firm. Merry and Grant have two children, a boy and a girl, and Marsha and Tim have twin daughters and a younger son."

"And Matt?" He smiled as he asked the question, admitting that he still remembered the battles between Melinda and her brother yet was well aware of the bond neither could deny.

Melinda reflected on how odd it seemed that Griff could be a stranger one moment and her old friend the next. Was he wrong about the boy she'd known being gone forever? Was there still a bit of her Savage left behind the respectable-attorney facade? "Matt's co-owner of a vacation resort in Tennessee," she said at last, remembering that Griff had asked her a question. "He's married to a wonderful woman, Brooke, who has become one of my closest friends as well as my sister-in-law. They have a daughter."

Griff rolled his eyes expressively, amusement making them gleam behind the polished lenses of his glasses. "Matt with a daughter? There should be some interesting battles in *that* household in a few years."

She couldn't help laughing in response. "Will there ever. He's mellowed a bit since you knew him, thanks mostly to Brooke, but he's still pretty much the same Matt. Very fond of having his own way, still sure his way is the best. Rachel, their daughter, is only four, but she's already proving to be just like him, with a bit of her equally stubborn and independent mother thrown in. I've already told him that I'm going to stand in her corner and serve as cheerleader when the battles begin."

"I'm sure he appreciated that," Griff commented dryly.

"He told me if I stuck my nose into his family business, he'd alter its placement on my face," Melinda replied with a grin.

Griff's eyes lingered for a moment on her nose. "That *would* be a shame," he commented, then looked away when the waiter arrived with their dinners.

Oddly shaken, Melinda stared at her plate, trying to remember what she'd ordered. Wondering if she would be able to taste it. She hadn't expected the attraction she'd felt for Griff Taylor from the first to continue to grow despite their differences. But all it took was an exchange of glances to add fuel to those banked flames.

"So you're the only one in your family who hasn't married." Griff looked at his plate as he spoke.

"I haven't found the man I could imagine waking up with every morning for the rest of my life," she answered candidly.

He shot her an unreadable look. "Any close prospects?"

"There've been a few. But none of them was the right one."

"So, you think you'll find that guy? And will you know when you do?"

"I'll find him," she answered certainly. "And I'll know. But in the meantime, I'm in no hurry. I like my life the way it is. I love my work, I enjoy my friends, and I have my brother and sisters and nieces and nephews when I need to be with family. I'm very happy."

"I'm glad to hear that." He seemed sincere.

During dinner, Melinda tried to learn more about the changes Griff had been through in the past few years.

"You've never returned to Springfield." It wasn't a question; she knew for a fact that he had not.

"No. There was nothing there for me but bad memories."

"Some people thought you'd come home for your father's funeral." She tried not to let her voice indicate that she'd been one of those people. Judging from the set of his mouth, she decided she hadn't been entirely successful.

"I was on an aircraft carrier half a world away when he died."

"You could have gotten leave—flown home."

He looked directly at her. "You're the one who pointed out recently that you can't stand hypocrites. Attending my father's funeral while still bearing the scars he gave me in his drunken rages would have been the most hypocritical thing I could have done."

Swallowing hard, she nodded her reluctant agreement. "When did you decide to become a lawyer?"

Griff shrugged. "A couple of years after I left Springfield."

"I thought you wanted to be a Navy pilot."

He shrugged again. "I realized pretty quickly that I didn't want to stay in the service that long—too restricting. So I attended college at night, put in my time then went to law school as soon as I got out. It took a bit longer than average. Dyson hired me right out of law school."

"You've made amazing progress with Dyson, I understand."

"I suppose you can say he likes my style," Griff said lightly, his eyes daring her to make a derogatory comment—or a remark about Dyson's eligible daughter.

Just the thought of Leslie Dyson reminded her of how slim the chances were that her attraction to this man could lead to anything but disappointment. "Do you like your work?" she asked instead, her tone implying that she found it hard to believe he could.

He gave the question a moment of consideration before answering. "I find the law fascinating. It's interesting to me how many interpretations there can be of the same words. I enjoy the challenge of taking a shaky case and winning. And I like the pay."

Ignoring the last, she asked quietly. "Is it true that you're going to represent Stanley Schulz in the East Plaza cases?"

His expression went blank, but he nodded. "Yes."

Her fingers tightened around her fork. "How can you keep doing that?" she demanded, genuinely puzzled. "How can you defend people who place money ahead of lives? The newspapers say that a sprinkler system in that building would very likely have saved all six of the people who died in that fire."

"At the time that office complex was built, there was no law requiring the installation of sprinkler systems," Griff told her flatly.

"The building was constructed less than two years before the law went into effect, when it was already becoming common practice to install them. And, according to the fire marshall's comments in the newspapers, Schulz had been advised many times in the past few years to have them installed," she retorted. "He didn't because he didn't want to spend the money—even though he could well afford it. Just as DayCo could have afforded adequate maintenance of the vacation cottage where poor Nancy Hawlsey nearly died," she added pointedly.

Setting his fork down with a precise, controlled movement, Griff met her eyes. "I'm not at liberty to discuss my cases with you, Melinda. I would assume you'd know that."

"You don't have the stomach to discuss them, you mean." She pushed her plate away, appetite gone. "You used to have so many ideals, so many principles. You got into who knows how many fights protecting weak or unpopular kids from the local bullies. You were even arrested for protesting the treatment of those two black teenagers who were beaten up by four bigoted cops. What happened to you?"

"How many times do I have to tell you that people change?" he asked in exasperation. "Look around, Melinda. The flower children have grown up to become stockbrokers and PTA presidents. The protest songs I listened to are used now to sell station wagons and athletic shoes. And I'm on a different side of the law than I used to be."

He took a deep breath, apparently intended to restore his control. "Do you have any idea how many frivolous personal-injury cases are filed every day in this country? The monumental waste of the court's time and the taxpayer's money? Medical treatment is almost unaffordable for the average citizen because the doctors have to be so heavily insured against malpractice cases. Hell, when some drunk falls down in a restaurant, sixteen lawyers urge him to sue because the carpet had a raised pattern in it that caused him to lose his balance! A baby's born with a genetic birth defect, the parents sue the doctor for not somehow knowing in advance that there would be problems, even though modern medicine hasn't gotten to a point of eliminating all birth defects yet, unfortunately. Insurance rates have climbed sky-high for the average business because juries keep awarding higher and higher judgments."

"Thanks to lawyers," Melinda interjected in a mutter.

"Yeah, well, Miss Hawlsey wasn't representing herself in that courtroom last week," he reminded her grimly. "Arthur Dayton deserved legal representation every bit as much as your friend did. And so does Stanley Schulz."

"And what about the truly innocent victims of corporate or medical negligence? People like Nancy Hawlsey? People like the six who died in that office fire? People like the woman who died on an operating table because her doctor was high on the controlled narcotics he'd become addicted to?"

"As I said, they deserve to be fairly represented. That's why we have a court system, because there are two sides to every case. It's up to the attorneys to best present their clients' arguments and the juries to decide who is the innocent party."

"Everyone is entitled to the best defense money can buy," she grumbled, paraphrasing a line from "The Big Easy."

His answer was the half shrug that had obviously become a habit since she'd known him before. "That's right. You want to talk about quack psychologists? Those who use their jobs to get laid on the pretense of offering sexual therapy? The ones who declare a patient mentally stable and release him from treatment, only to have that same patient go on a shooting rampage two weeks later?"

She glowered, knowing better than to argue with him. Griff had become too good at arguing. She knew she couldn't win, despite the heated words trembling on the end of her tongue. "Maybe we'd better change the subject."

"Perhaps we'd better. You seem to have lost interest in your dinner. Would you like some dessert?"

"No, thank you."

"Then I'll take you home."

"Fine."

"WE CAN'T SEEM TO GET ALONG any more, can we?" Melinda heard the wistfulness in her voice as they stood inside her apartment, the door open. Griff was obviously poised to leave as quickly as possible. The ride home hadn't been a comfortable one, though they'd tried to make innocuous conversation. For some reason, small talk just didn't work for them.

One hand braced on the doorjamb, the other in his pocket, Griff grimaced. "We do seem to clash a bit."

She toyed with her beads, looking solemnly at him. "I never thought it would be like this between us. We were once so close. Remember the night I cried in your arms because I missed my mom so much, and you broke down because you were still so angry with your own mother for walking out on you?"

His dark eyes went bleak. "Some memories are best left in the past, Melinda."

"Some refuse to stay buried," she whispered, knowing she'd never forget that night, no matter how many years would pass. A raw, devastating wound had begun to heal then, one that her loving siblings and caring minister hadn't been able to ease. The others had treated the grief, but not the deep-seated anger. Only Savage had seemed to comprehend how angry she'd been at the circumstances that had robbed her of her parents at such a young, vulnerable age. He'd carried enough anger of his own to recognize the emotion that even Melinda hadn't acknowledged until he'd helped her understand it. "Have you forgotten everything between us, Griff?"

"Not everything," he admitted roughly. "I remember the night I kissed you. It was the night I decided to join the Navy and get out of town—just a few weeks before I graduated from high school."

Her eyes widened, her cheeks warming a bit at the reminder of that first, sweet kiss. It seemed hard to believe that this tall, hard man in front of her had given that kiss. "That was when you decided to leave? Why?"

He hesitated, then looked ruefully at her. "You were fourteen. I was only a month away from eighteen. At the time, the few years between us made quite a difference. I was ready for a more...mature relationship. You weren't."

She smiled sadly. "At the time, I wasn't even sure what a more mature relationship was."

"I know."

"Ironic, isn't it?" she mused. "Twelve years ago, our ages kept us apart when otherwise we were a wonderful pair. Now that our ages are right, we're too different to be together."

He looked as though he wanted to argue—but only for a moment. "I suppose you're right," he admitted at length. "You despise what I do, and I'm not comfortable with the memories you bring back."

"I can't help reminding you of your past."

"And I can't change what I am."

It was as if they agreed that whatever sparks had ignited between them were to be doused before they could develop into possibly devastating flames. Melinda admired his subtlety even as she admitted to herself that she was rather disappointed it had to be this way. She agreed, however. Something told her that this new and not necessarily improved Griff Taylor would only bring heartache should she allow things to go any further between them. "Thanks for the dinner, Griff. It was nice to get together again."

His wince told her how inadequate he found her words, but he only nodded. "Good night, then. Maybe we'll see each other around."

"Yeah. Maybe."

"So—um—" Awkwardness sat uncomfortably on this man who'd become so effortlessly self-assured. "Good night," he repeated.

"Good night, Griff."

She stared pensively at the door for several long moments after it closed behind him. And then she turned to head for her bedroom, deciding to take a long, quiet bath and make an effort to sort out her tangled feelings for Griff Taylor.

She'd taken only a step when the impatient rap on the door made her freeze. She knew even as she opened it who would be standing on the other side. "Did you forget something?"

Griff glared enigmatically at her. "Yeah." The word was clipped. "This is going to drive me crazy if I don't do something about it. Call it curiosity."

"What are you—" The puzzled question died on her lips when he reached for her. "Griff, you can't—"

He did. His mouth covered hers before she could finish speaking.

That first kiss had been a long time before. The details had faded to sweet, hazy memory. There'd been many kisses since—some that she'd considered spectacular. So what was it about this one that jolted her all the way down to her heels?

He wasn't gentle, or tentative, or even particularly considerate. The kiss was rough, hot, deep. He demonstrated quite clearly that he no longer considered her an innocent to be treated with careful restraint. She was a woman he found desirable—even if that desire was unwelcome. And he made her want him—or had she wanted him since she'd seen him standing in the courtroom, even before she'd known who he was?

By the time he pulled away, Melinda was a quivering mass of jelly. Griff didn't appear to be in much better shape. "Now we know," he muttered, shoving both hands into his pockets.

"Know what?" she managed, her voice little more than a squeak.

"What it could be like between us if things were different. Good night, Melinda."

The door closed behind him again, and this time she knew he wouldn't be back. It took her a moment to trust her legs. And then she turned and headed for the bathroom, thinking that maybe a cold shower would be better than a hot bath, after all.

That hadn't been a conservative, repressed attorney who'd kissed her. That had been a grown-up, still dangerous version of a boy who'd once called himself Savage. And that was a man with whom she could imagine a future.

She had a great deal to think about—after her shower.

"SO HE REALLY WAS THE BOY you knew from school." Fred shook his head in amazement. "Imagine that. Griffin Taylor, a guy called Savage who stayed in trouble with the law? I never would have guessed."

"Fred, you won't mention this to anyone, will you? He really doesn't want his past made public. Promise me you won't say anything."

Fred gave her a look that spoke volumes. "Melinda, I'm a psychologist, remember? I know how to keep a secret."

She smiled her apology. "I know you do. Sorry."

"Forgiven. This time. So you're not going to see him again?"

"He doesn't think so. I haven't decided."

Fred grinned. "Now that's my Melinda."

Pulling idly at a thick curl, she pursed her lips in thought, her eyes on the spotted ceiling of her office as she leaned back in her desk chair, sneakered feet propped on her desk. "If there's even a chance that Savage still lives inside that tame, rabidly right-wing body..." Her voice trailed off. She wasn't sure how she'd intended to finish the sentence. Unconsciously, her fingertip moved slowly over lips that still seemed to tingle from a kiss that had shaken her to her core.

Fred sounded rather worried when he spoke again. "Just how hung up are you on this memory, Melinda? If you're hoping to base a relationship on feelings you had when you were fourteen, you're doomed for disappointment. You realize that, don't you?"

"The problem with working with shrinks all day," she commented with a gusty sigh, still gazing at the ceiling, "is that you wind up being analyzed at least once every hour." She looked at him. "No, Fred, I'm not hung up on a memory. To be perfectly honest, I'm very much attracted to the Griff Taylor I had dinner with Saturday night. But, unless there's more to him than meets the eye, the two of us are all wrong for each other. There has to be some common ground, you know?"

"And if there's not?"

She shrugged in unconscious imitation of Griff. "Then there's not."

"So how are you going to find out? He's not interested in seeing you again, remember?"

"I didn't say he wasn't interested," Melinda disputed immediately, frowning. "He just doesn't think it would be wise, and he doesn't deliberately do foolish things these days."

"So what are you going to do?" Fred repeated patiently.

Her smile was one any member of her family would have recognized—and groaned in misgiving at the sight of. The family had agreed some time earlier that Melinda-with-a-purpose was a frightening prospect. "I suppose I'll just have to arrange to see him again and find out for myself if there's hope for him yet."

Fred's left eyebrow rose slowly in an expressive gesture Melinda had long coveted. "And just how are you going to arrange that without him knowing what you're doing?"

Her chin tilted arrogantly. "My dearest partner, have you no faith? Haven't I told you the story of how I arranged for my brother and his then-future wife to get back together after they'd had a terrible fight? And what about—"

Her friend held up a hasty hand to stop her. "Now don't start with all the stories of your brilliant scheming again. I'm well aware of your ability to manipulate yourself out of—or into—any situation if you so desire. I only asked if you have a plan this time."

"The germs of one."

"Germs is the right term," Fred murmured. "Some of your schemes are downright sick."

She laughed. "Oh, come on. I'm not that bad."

He faked a choking cough.

"Well, not all the time," she amended humorously. "Go away, Fred. I have a patient due in fifteen minutes. I need to prepare myself."

Standing, he glanced at her appointment book, then winced. "Oh, Lord. Not Mr. Peterson. Another whole hour of his whining about how terribly his vicious wife mistreats him and all the reasons he can't seem to get away from her."

Melinda lifted her hands. "One of these days, one of us is going to convince him that he really loves that old shrew or he would have been gone a long time ago. In the meantime he just wants a sympathetic ear—and he's lost you and Murphy."

"We ran out of sympathy," Fred agreed. "You just wait. You will, too."

"Maybe not. Maybe I'll be the one to get through to him."

"I hope so, kid. For his sake and yours, I hope so. See you later."

"Yeah. Later." Melinda spoke distractedly, her thoughts already shifting away from her partner and her patient.

A plan, she thought. *I need a plan*. Her mouth tilted into the beginnings of a smile as ideas began to swirl within her notoriously devious head.

GRIFF WAS TRYING to have a good time. He really was. After all, he'd be spending a great deal of time at important charity functions like this one if things continued as they had been for the past two years. And he'd be spending a great deal of time with the woman at his side if Wallace Dyson had his way.

Glancing at Leslie's pretty though not particularly notable face, Griff reminded himself that marriage to her hadn't seemed like such a terrible idea when he'd first realized what Dyson had in mind. Leslie was attractive, pleasant enough company, trained from birth to be exactly the type of corporate wife Griff needed to advance his image of up-and-coming young attorney with political potential.

If there was little fire in the relationship, if passion was conspicuously absent, well, he'd convinced himself that didn't particularly matter. He'd learned long ago not to place much faith in strong emotions. Financial and social success were attained with the head, not through the heart. When the time came to make love with Leslie, he was quite sure he'd find the right incentive.

So why had he spent the evening smiling at the blue-eyed brunette at his side and trying not to think of a certain green-eyed strawberry blonde?

Dammit, he had to put Melinda James out of his mind—and out of his life. Again. He'd left her long ago for her own sake as well as his. He had to do the same thing now. They were hopelessly wrong for each other, despite the magnetism that seemed to exist between them.

He'd spent the past week trying to tell himself that they were drawn to each other only because of their history. But it wasn't a fourteen-year-old girl he remembered in the middle of the night; it hadn't been a memory he'd held in his arms. His most uncomfortable memories now were much more recent—a week old, to be exact. The way her slender body had molded itself to his. The feel of her curves through a clinging satin dress. The taste of her. The fire of her response to him.

He'd been fond of the child. He wanted the woman with a hunger that was new to him.

And he didn't know what in hell he was going to do about it.

The wisest thing to do, he reminded himself sternly, was to stay away from her. Just as he'd been doing for the past week, though it had been harder than he'd expected, knowing she was only a matter of minutes away. But he prided himself on his willpower. He hadn't seen her again and he wouldn't. She was out of his life, and now all he had to do was get her out of his mind.

"Griff, didn't you hear me? I'm thirsty. I'd like a drink, please."

"Oh, sorry, Leslie. I was thinking about something else. What would you—"

He never finished the sentence. Five feet away from him, dressed in a shimmery silver sheath that clung lovingly to every bewitching curve, stood Melinda James, her hand resting lightly on the arm of a tall, auburn-haired man, her wickedly uptilted emerald eyes locked in challenge with Griff's.

4

MELINDA HAD AGREED to attend the charity auction and dance several weeks in advance, before the unexpected reunion with Griff. Then she'd found out from her reliable inside source—Fred—that Griff would be attending with Leslie Dyson, and she'd decided there was no time like the present to begin her campaign to reveal the *real* Griffin Taylor.

Now that she was face to face with Griff and his date, she wasn't quite sure how to proceed. A trained, professional psychologist should be above cattiness, she told herself firmly, her glance skidding off the woman at Griff's side. Wouldn't notice that Leslie Dyson's light green dress did little to flatter her pale complexion and dark hair. Wouldn't revel in the flare of...of something dangerous in Griff's expression as he stared at Melinda. Dangerous—and thrillingly exciting.

"Why, hello, Griff," she murmured, looking straight into his smoldering eyes. "And Leslie. How nice to see you again."

Leslie's smooth brow creased in momentary thought. Melinda tried to suppress the ignoble mental voice that pointed out what a difficult task thinking seemed to be for the pretty brunette. She was disappointed in herself for reverting to bitchy adolescence simply because she was jealous that another woman clung to Griff Taylor's well-developed biceps.

Jealous? Acknowledging the unfamiliar emotion, she sighed imperceptibly. What in the world was happening to her?

Her frown vanishing, Leslie smiled warmly, and Melinda felt even guiltier. "Of course. You're Melinda James," Leslie murmured in her finishing-school accent. "We met at the cystic fibrosis benefit last month. You know Griff?"

Trust Leslie not to be aware that Melinda had been a damaging witness against her father's law firm. Melinda wondered in exasperation if the woman ever read any section of the newspaper other than the society pages.

Before Melinda could respond to Leslie's question, Griff spoke. "We've met," he said a bit too bluntly. Pulling off his glasses to dangle them from one hand, he looked pointedly at the tall, slender man who stood at Melinda's side, seemingly quite amused by the silent interplay between Griff and Melinda. Griff seemed particularly annoyed by the yellow and orange flowered cummerbund Murphy had chosen to wear with an otherwise conventional black tux. "Your date, Melinda?"

She tried to interpret the edge in his voice. It was too much to hope that he was also fighting the green-eyed monster. Wasn't it? She slipped a hand beneath Murphy's arm, earning a laughing look of censure from her friend and partner. "Leslie Dyson, Griff Taylor, this is Murphy Ryan."

Murphy smiled at Leslie, then extended a hand to Griff. "So you're the attorney who had Melinda chewing the furniture at the clinic a few weeks ago. It must have been an interesting battle for the court spectators. I understand your client lost."

Mentally groaning at Murphy's wicked sense of humor and total disregard for polite niceties, Melinda tried to smile at the look Griff gave her partner. The handshake was notably brief. And then Griff turned to Melinda, his gaze lingering for a moment on the deep V of her slinky silver dress before dropping to the thigh-high slit in the skirt. "I hear they're auctioning some very nice items this evening," he commented a bit gruffly, obviously trying to make innocuous social small talk, very deliberately ignoring Murphy's comments.

"Yes, the local merchants were quite generous in their donations," Melinda agreed blandly. Griff's respectable facade was quite firmly in place, she noted, almost irresistibly tempted to test it. "I'm sure the auction will be very profitable for Hope House." Hope House was a local workshop for developmentally disabled adults, and a very worthwhile cause in Melinda's opinion. She intended to bid on a few of the items herself, knowing her money would be well spent.

"Quite an evening, isn't it?" Murphy contributed, his eyes glinting mischievously. "All the good people here to benefit charity, dripping in jewels and so stylishly dressed."

"Or so stylishly *un*dressed," Griff muttered, gaze straying again to Melinda's daring décolletage.

"What a prudish remark." Melinda trusted that she sounded more detached than she felt. She hoped the thin, clinging fabric somehow managed to conceal the way her heart hammered against her ribs.

Griff's eyes met hers and for a moment she glimpsed again that flare of danger lurking deeply within the tame, civilized exterior. Just a flash of the primitive male who'd turned her to putty with only a kiss. Her pounding heart seemed to stop.

And then Leslie tugged at Griff's arm, reminding Melinda of an impatient child. "Griff, I'm still thirsty. And people are beginning to be seated for the auction."

Instantly the danger was gone, replaced by an indulgent smile that set Melinda's teeth on edge. Griff slipped his glasses on his nose and straightened them with one finger, donning his bland, Clark Kent facade, Melinda reflected irritably. "All right, Leslie. I'll get you some champagne. Why don't you go ahead and find seats for us close to the front."

Melinda couldn't help noting that Griff's tone was one he might well have used with a rather spoiled child. He'd never spoken to *her* that way, even when he'd known her at fourteen. She'd probably have decked him if he had, she acknowledged. He didn't look at her again, but gave a rather brusque nod and turned toward the bar.

She'd never know how long she would have remained in the same spot had Murphy not taken her arm and firmly turned her toward the auction room. "Mustn't be caught staring after him," he chided her humorously. "Ruins that cool, snooty image you were putting on for him."

Flushing in annoyance—more at herself than Murphy—Melinda tossed her heavy blond mane and glared at her partner. "I *wasn't* staring after him. I was just—um—thinking about something."

"Uh-huh. And I know exactly what you were thinking about."

Melinda slanted him a warning look. "Watch it, Ryan. You don't really want me to lose my temper right here among the cream of society, do you?"

He chuckled, slinging an arm loosely around her bare shoulders. "Heaven forbid. Not that."

"Then belt up."

"Hey, no problem. So, what are you bidding on tonight?"

She knew exactly what she wanted and was aware of the rather dismal condition of her bank account at the moment. Though money was not a problem for her family, Melinda had made quite an issue of living on her own means. Since she'd chosen counseling in a small clinic as a career, she'd realized that she'd never make a huge salary. She'd convinced herself years earlier that, despite her deep appreciation for the luxuries money could provide, wealth was not as important to her as a sense of accomplishment. There were times, however. . . .

"A tea service," she murmured wistfully in answer to Murphy's question.

"Yeah? What kind?"

"I'd love to have a nice china service for the office. You know how I love to have tea between appointments, and I've never been too crazy about that ceramic set I have now. I heard there are several china tea services being auctioned tonight."

Looking skeptical, Murphy grimaced. "Yeah, but at what prices?"

Melinda made a face. "I know. They'll probably be exorbitant. But I'm still going to try for one."

"Good luck."

"Thanks." Her hand tucked comfortably into her friend's arm, Melinda walked with him into the auction room, trying to concentrate on the tea service and not on that exciting expression in Griff's eyes when he'd looked at her.

THE TEA SERVICE was exactly what she'd imagined. The sleek, undecorated set was made of pearl-gray bone china. A teapot, two cups, sugar bowl and creamer rested on a matching tray that she could already feel between her hands. Picturing herself sipping tea from one of the dainty cups, she knew she had to have it— as long as the bidding didn't go over the hundred fifty dollars she'd set as her limit for the evening.

"I want it," she muttered to Murphy, feeling the adrenaline rush that always preceded a battle.

He gave her a lopsided grin, apparently enjoying the expression of pure lust she knew she must be wearing. "How much?"

"One fifty. And if it gets any higher than that, put a hand over my mouth, will you?"

"Listen, Mel, I can donate a few dollars to the cause if necessary. If you want it that badly, we'll get it."

She shook her head firmly. "Thanks, Murph, but it's got to be something I buy for myself, you know?"

He tapped her firm chin with one finger. "You and that stubborn pride of yours. All right, I'll keep my wallet in my pocket. But am I allowed to glare a warning at anyone who bids against you?"

"Are you kidding? I want you to give them a look that has them shaking in their boots. I never said I had anything against winning by intimidation."

He laughed, earning a look of censure from the plump matron in front of them, who was trying to listen to the auctioneer as he accepted a four-hundred-dollar bid for a porcelain bud vase. Murphy's laugh also drew attention from another source. Griff, seated with Leslie across the aisle from Melinda and Murphy, had been glaring at them for the past hour. Melinda hadn't quite been able to interpret those looks, but she was beginning to enjoy them. There was something exhilarating about taunting Griffin Taylor, despite her certainty that she was flirting with danger. Perhaps because of that certainty.

When Melinda's gaze clashed with Griff's, he looked away, turning his attention pointedly toward the front. Melinda's eyes lingered on his stern profile for only a moment before she, too, looked forward as the auctioneer described the tea service she'd spotted moments before. She lifted her numbered card for attention when the auctioneer opened the bidding at twenty-five dollars.

"I have twenty-five, do I hear thirty? Thirty dollars? Thirty. Do I have thirty-five?"

Full concentration on the auctioneer, Melinda raised her card.

"Thirty-five. Do I have forty? Thank you, forty. And forty-five. Do I have fifty?"

Melinda waved her card.

"Fifty. Fifty-five. Sixty. Give me sixty-five. Sixty-five. Now what about seventy?"

Swallowing hard, Melinda bid seventy, still with a silent determination that blinded her to everything but the auctioneer and the coveted tea service.

The bidding had risen to one hundred ten—Melinda's bid—before she realized that Murphy was chuckling heartily, if quietly, beside her. "What's so funny?" she hissed, still looking frontward.

"Don't you know who you're bidding against?" His voice rippled with laughter. "Everyone else has dropped out."

"Everyone else but who?" she asked, finally glancing his way. And then she froze when, across the aisle, Griff discreetly lifted his number, raising the bid to one hundred twenty-dollars. "Why, that—" She scowled at Murphy. "He's bidding against me!"

"I don't think he's realized it yet, either." Murphy seemed barely able to contain a burst of laughter. "You'd better raise the bid if you're still in the running."

"You bet I'm in the running." Grimly, Melinda shoved her card into the air.

"One twenty-five," the auctioneer announced smoothly, nodding at her. "Do I have one fifty? One fifty?"

"One thirty-five," Griff offered, the first audible bid for that particular item.

"Thank you, one thirty-five. One thirty-five—"

"One forty," Melinda called out in challenge.

Her attention was on Griff when he swiveled his head abruptly at the sound of her voice. Their eyes locked. His narrowed. "One forty-five."

Melinda didn't hesitate. "One fifty."

"One sixty."

"Thank you," began the auctioneer, "do I—"

"One seventy," Melinda announced clearly. She wanted that tea service. Now more than before.

"Uh, Melinda—" Murphy whispered. She ignored him.

"One eighty," Griff responded.

The audience was beginning to enjoy the contest unfolding before them, the first bit of excitement in an otherwise routine charity event. Heads swayed from left to right, much as they would at a tennis match, as the bidding climbed higher. The auctioneer was becoming superfluous, barely having time to acknowledge each bid before the next was issued.

"Melinda," Murphy tried again when the price rose to two hundred dollars. "Weren't you—"

"Two hundred twenty," she pronounced. Murphy groaned and slumped in his seat.

"Two-fifty," Griff said smoothly, ignoring Leslie's tug at his sleeve.

Melinda paused. And then she pictured *her* lovely tea service sitting in Griff's coolly trendy office. His heartless, greedy clients sipping tea from *her* delicate cups. "Three hundred," she snapped. There was always her savings account.

"Three twenty-five."

She'd been angrier. She'd been more determined to have her own way. She just couldn't remember any such occasion at the moment. "Three fifty."

Murphy hid his face in his hands, shoulders shaking. Appalled by the fascinated attention they were receiving, Leslie was red-faced as she tried to melt into the back of her seat. As though there was no one else in the room, Griff glared at Melinda. "Three seventy-five."

She could always call her brother for a loan. Wouldn't Matt love *that*, she thought, even as she spoke. "Four."

If Griff sat any straighter, he'd be standing. His expression now was the same one he wore in court. Predator. Fighter. One who wasn't accustomed to losing. "Seven hundred dollars." The words were spoken quietly, but everyone in the room heard them quite clearly. The audience gasped.

Melinda drew a deep breath, only to hold it when a large hand clamped over her mouth. Furiously she began to struggle, but then Murphy turned her face so that she was looking at him. "Melinda," he said firmly. "Seven. Hundred. Dollars."

Seven hundred dollars. She gulped and went boneless, feeling her eyes round as the amount penetrated the red haze that seemed to have gripped her for the past ten minutes or so. *Seven hundred dollars?*

A titter of restrained laughter underscored the auctioneer's delighted chatter. "Seven hundred. Do I hear seven fifty?"

Melinda swallowed and nodded for Murphy to remove his hand, which he did warily, obviously prepared to clap it right back if she so much as opened her mouth. She sat mutely, resentful eyes turning toward Griff.

"Seven hundred going once . . . twice . . . sold to the gentleman for seven hundred dollars. And Hope House thanks you for that very generous donation, sir."

For the rest of her life Melinda would cherish the look on Griff's face when he suddenly understood exactly what he'd done. Smug victory turned to annoyed consternation when he realized that he'd just paid seven hundred dollars for a tea service that would retail for perhaps three hundred. Melinda wasn't the only one to laugh at his expression. Holding her side, she buried her face in Murphy's shoulder to restrain herself as the auctioneer moved to the next item. "His face," she managed finally in a breathless whisper. "Oh, Murph, did you see his face?"

"Um, Melinda, you'd better stop giggling. If you could see his face *now* . . ."

She shook her head stubbornly. "I don't care. And I don't dare look at him now or I'll fall out of my chair laughing and embarrass all of us."

"Now she worries about embarrassing me," Murphy murmured to no one in particular.

Melinda giggled again, then sat straighter, controlling herself with some effort. She resisted all temptation to look at Griff again during the auction, even when she bid on and bought an antique cookie tin and an inexpensive, cheerfully garish rhinestone clip for her hair. She had a feeling she'd be facing him soon enough.

THE BAND WAS EXCELLENT. Murphy was a wonderful dance partner. Melinda was having a marvelous time.

"Aren't we proud of ourselves?" Murphy teased, dipping her over one arm at the end of a particularly lively dance.

"Why, Murphy." She batted her eyelashes and tried to look innocent as she dangled two feet above the floor. "I have no idea what you mean."

He laughed and set her upright. "You brat. Someone should have taken a paddle to you years ago."

Her brow lifted imperiously. "You're not the only one who's mentioned that lately." But Murphy's laughing comment didn't annoy her nearly as much as Griff had when he'd semiseriously suggested the same thing.

"Now why doesn't that surprise me?" Murphy grinned at her, then made a production of gulping noisily. "Uh, Melinda. Guess who's coming. . . ."

She didn't have to guess. The hairs at the back of her neck had already warned her that Griff was in the vicinity. She wasn't quite sure how he managed it, but moments later she found herself in his arms, being forcefully whirled across the floor just as Murphy invited Leslie to dance.

"Was I asked if I wanted to dance?" Melinda inquired of the air over Griff's shoulder. "And if so, why do I feel as though I was kidnapped?"

Ignoring her question, Griff glared at her. "Are you proud of yourself?"

"In general or over anything in particular?"

"You know exactly what I mean," he snapped. "You made a fool of me in there."

"No, Griff," she assured him gravely, "I would definitely say that you are a self-made man."

"You manipulated me. If it hadn't been for you, I—"

"Listen, Griffin Taylor," she interrupted, fed up with his scolding. "*I* made the first bid on that set. I didn't even know you were in the bidding until just before you spoke. You're the one who immediately turned it into some sort of battle. And you're the one who upped the price by three hundred dollars just so you could win. Explain *that!*"

His lean cheeks darkened a bit, his eyes smoldering. "Well, I—"

"Maybe there's still more of your old self inside that young-attorney facade than you like to admit," she dared recklessly. "Maybe you're still the same old Savage—the guy who could never resist a challenge."

"Wrong. What you saw was the new me. The man who doesn't like to lose, and who'll do anything necessary to assure a win. That's what you claim not to like about me now, remember?"

She stroked one finger along the back of his neck, following his dancing effortlessly. "So what would you say if I told you that I liked you more during that auction than I have since we saw each other again?"

He looked grim. "I'd say I was sorry to hear it. Whatever happened in there isn't going to happen again. Maybe I got carried away, but from now on I'm going to stay in control. I am not going to allow you to disrupt the life I've made for myself, Melinda James."

Rounding her eyes innocently, Melinda stared at him, her fingers slipping into the crisp hair at the back of his head as she moved almost imperceptibly closer to him. "Why, Griff, would I try to disrupt your life?"

If she hadn't felt his heart pounding against her unbound breasts, she might have been intimidated by the look he gave her.

"Now what are you doing?" Griff said abruptly.

The next movement of the dance brought her in sinuous contact with him as they made a tight turn. She accidentally brushed her hair against his jaw as she looked up at him in question. "I beg your pardon?"

"Melinda. Stop it."

"Stop what, Griff?"

"Playing dumb. It doesn't become you."

She fluttered her lashes, sliding her other hand up his strong chest until both hands rested behind his head. "I thought maybe that was the way you like women to act around you," she murmured, unable to resist just one ignoble dig at his date.

Dark brows lowering behind his glasses, he reached behind his head to catch her right hand in his left, holding it in a more conservative dance position. "Yeah? And what about you? Have your tastes turned to grinning clowns in flowered cummerbunds?"

She tossed her head, offended on Murphy's behalf. "I'll have you know that Murphy has a doctorate in psychology, a second doctorate in family counseling and a master's in sociology. He's got an IQ higher than most people's bank balances and has been published in medical and psychological journals in six different languages. Of course, he's not from a distinguished moneyed family background, but then only the very snobby or very hypocritical care about that sort of thing."

"Are you sleeping with him?"

Melinda's mouth dropped open. Judging from the look on Griff's face, he seemed as surprised by the question as she was. Which didn't stop her from retorting angrily, "Are you sleeping with *her*?"

"No."

She hadn't really expected him to answer, but she felt incredible relief that he had. Dropping her eyes, she concentrated on her suddenly awkward feet. "Murphy and I are business partners and friends. That's all," she muttered.

"Melinda, I—"

This time it really was an accident that she almost stumbled, making his arms tighten abruptly around her to steady her. A whiff of air couldn't have passed between them as their eyes met, locked. "If you're trying to get yourself hauled out of here over my shoulder," he warned huskily, "you're doing a damned good job of it."

She couldn't prevent the trace of bitterness in her reply. "I might have believed that had I been dancing with Savage. Counselor Griffin Taylor would never do anything so impetuous. So scandalous."

He scowled. The music ended. Griff dropped his arms, the loss of his touch leaving Melinda feeling curiously bereft. "I'll take you back to your date." His voice was stiff, his expression unreadable.

She nodded unhappily, her seductive teasing suddenly losing its appeal. She'd been trying to find out more about Griff. All she'd succeeded in doing was fueling her growing desire for him. "All right."

Leslie and Murphy seemed to have gotten along quite well during their dance. Melinda wondered why she and Griff seemed so incapable of spending even a few moments without clashing. Murmuring appropriate responses as Griff and Leslie said their good-nights, she avoided Griff's eyes, turning to Murphy as soon as the other couple had departed. "Let's get out of here, okay?"

"Did you and Taylor go at each other again?" he asked sympathetically, walking with her toward the nearest exit.

"You could say that," she answered with a wince.

He waited until they'd belted themselves into his car before speaking again. "You know, Leslie's really quite nice," he commented carefully, eyes on the road as he turned toward her home. "I feel kind of sorry for her, actually. She appears to be a rather unhappy young woman whose primary purpose in life seems to be trying to please her overly demanding father."

Tugging at her lower lip, Melinda mused that she, too, could feel sorry for Leslie. And then she wondered just how far the other woman would go to please her father. Would she marry a man she didn't love? Or maybe Leslie *was* in love with Griff. Melinda couldn't find that too hard to believe.

Griffin Taylor was a man who'd be all too easy to love—if he were her type, she added hastily. But was he her type? She still didn't know the answer to that particular question. Perhaps she never would.

Perhaps it was too late to wonder.

5

THE PACKAGE ARRIVED at her office a week later. Something told her even before she ripped off the tape what she'd find inside. It had been delivered during a meeting between the clinic partners, so Murphy and Fred were both watching when she lifted the pearl-gray china teapot from its secure nest of packaging material.

"Now there's something that looks ominously familiar," Murphy commented, a spark of intrigue in his eyes.

Fred tilted his head, examining the teapot. "Not to me. Should it?"

"Remember the tea service I told you about?" Murphy asked.

Fred's eyes widened. "*That* tea service? The seven-hundred-dollar tea service?"

"It's only a china tea service, not sterling silver," Melinda interjected quietly, the first time she'd been able to speak since opening the box.

"For which Griffin Taylor paid seven hundred dollars," Murphy added.

Fred stroked his jaw. "You'd think someone who wanted it that badly would hang onto it for a bit longer than a week."

"Why do you suppose he sent it to her?" Murphy pointedly ignored Melinda as he looked gravely at his other partner.

"Could it be love?"

"I suppose it could be. But, remembering the look on his face when that auction ended, I wouldn't drink anything from that pot if I were you. Is it possible to poison china?"

Fred chuckled. "Interesting question. Perhaps we should have it analyzed by the closest medical lab."

Melinda tapped her foot noisily against her chair. "If you two adolescents are quite finished . . ."

"Fred, old boy, I believe she's becoming annoyed."

"You just may be correct, old chum. Note the high color in her porcelain cheeks. The sparks in her gorgeous green eyes. The—"

Melinda interrupted with a few well-chosen words.

"—the profanities issuing from her rosebud mouth," Murphy murmured with a grin.

Melinda stood, swinging an arm dramatically toward the door. "Out."

"D'you suppose she means *us?*" Fred inquired.

"Get . . . out."

"I think she does," Murphy concurred.

"Now!"

"Meeting adjourned," Fred announced hastily when Melinda picked up a thick notebook, hefting it in warning.

Murphy was right behind Fred when he escaped through the doorway, but couldn't seem to resist poking his head around the edge of the door. "Thank the man nicely, Melinda," he admonished, his expression devilish.

The door closed only a moment before the notebook hit it full force.

Sinking into her chair, Melinda stared at the teapot resting innocently on her desk. Why had he sent it? Was the gift meant to please her? Or to taunt her?

Or was it another of those reminders of her that he wanted out of his life?

At least he hadn't included the little wooden plaque, she thought, when the second possibility threatened to depress her. Maybe the tea service really was intended to please her.

An apology, maybe, for the way he'd chewed her out about his impulsive behavior during the auction?

She emptied the box, carefully setting the contents on her desk as she searched fruitlessly for a card. Nothing. Not that there'd been any doubt as to who sent the set. But an explanation would have been nice.

She reached for the phone and dialed the number of his office.

"Griffin Taylor, please," she said when an emotionless voice answered. "This is Melinda James."

"One moment, please. I'll see if he's in."

Making a face at the elevator music pouring into her ear during the next few minutes, Melinda waited for Griff to pick up the line. He would if he was available, she decided. He'd know she would demand an explanation.

"Taylor."

His deep, rich voice made her shiver, but her voice came out normally enough. "Hi, it's me."

"I know."

She twisted the phone cord around one scarlet-nailed finger, suddenly groping for words. She finally settled for a straight question. "Why'd you send it?"

"You wanted it, didn't you?"

"So did you."

"Yeah, well, I decided it didn't match my office, after all."

She frowned at her booted toes. "A pretty expensive mistake, wasn't it?"

"I can write it off, remember? Charity."

Her chin firmed. What was his game now? "I'm no charity case. I'll send you a check first thing next week." And just where was she supposed to come up with seven hundred dollars?

"You do and you'll receive an envelope of confetti by return mail. The tea set is a gift, Melinda. I want you to have it."

"Why?" she repeated, refusing to accept his arguments.

He sighed. "Call it a peace offering."

"I—um—" What else could she say? "Thank you."

"You're welcome."

There was a long pause. Melinda tried desperately to think of something witty, something clever to say. She'd never had trouble coming up with those offhand, even reckless remarks before. Why was she suddenly tongue-tied now? Why did the next few moments seem so terribly important?

As it happened, Griff was the one to break the silence. "I want to see you again."

Her eyes closed, her fingers tightening on the cord. "You do?" She sounded much too breathless. Clearing her throat, she opened her eyes and tried again. "Why?"

"Dammit, what's with you and the whys today?" he exploded, obviously short-tempered. Melinda had to wonder if it was because of his confusion about her. "I just do, okay? I don't know why."

She tossed her head imperiously, the gesture wasted on the empty office. "That's not very flattering."

"Since when are you the kind who wants to be flattered? Will you see me or not?"

"Maybe," she replied, her confidence returning as Griff's seemed to falter. "Why don't you give me a call sometime?"

"Dammit, Melinda!"

"I have to go, Griff. I have a meeting to get back to. Thanks again for the tea service."

"Melinda, wait—"

But she'd already pulled the receiver away from her ear. She took a deep breath after she'd cradled it. She'd pay for that. Smiling secretly, she decided it would be worth it.

It was fun to tease a savage. Even a savage in a gentleman's clothing.

"DON'T YOU EVER ASK who's there before you open your door?" Griff demanded, then wished his opening words hadn't been a reprimand when Melinda immediately bristled.

"I never thought I'd say this, but you sound exactly like my brother," she accused, blocking the doorway to keep him outside. "And what are you doing here? You were supposed to call sometime."

"Believe me, Melinda, I have no intention of sounding like your brother. Are you going to let me in?"

"Do I have any choice? Last time you just pushed past me."

He shoved his hands in his pockets to keep them out of trouble. "You have a choice." Not that he intended to listen if she told him to leave.

She eyed him suspiciously, then snorted delicately. "Sure I do. I make my choice and then you do whatever you want, anyway." She sighed and stepped back. "What the hell. Come in, Griff."

Reluctantly amused by her exaggerated, resigned expression, he stepped past her. Waiting until she'd closed the door before speaking again, he ran his gaze hungrily over her. The beige T-shirt, jungle-print vest and baggy olive-green fatigue pants were hardly feminine attire, and yet on Melinda, they looked entirely feminine. But then, so would a potato sack, he decided, studying the soft curves beneath the sturdy clothing.

Her gaze met his, and he noted her expression. As if she knew exactly what he was thinking, he decided, uncomfortable with being read so easily. "Have dinner with me." He suddenly needed very badly to get out of the apartment. Being alone with her was too dangerous. His emotions were too unpredictable.

Her eyes taunted him. "And if I already have a date?"

He scowled. "Stop toying with me. Do you have a date or don't you?"

"No."

"Then—"

"All right. We'll have dinner. I could fix something here."

"No," he said a bit too quickly. "Let's go out."

Again, her eyes laughed at him. Dammit, he thought. This woman could push a saint to violence. So why the hell did he find her so utterly fascinating? And why did he want to make love to her even more than he wanted to turn her over his knee?

"Fine. I'll get my purse."

"Um—"

She paused when he spoke, her eyebrows lifted in question.

"Don't you want to change?" he hinted, motioning toward his impeccable dark suit, which emphasized her casual attire.

"No." The word was spoken lightly, but issued in unmistakable challenge.

His teeth ground together. "Fine. Get your purse."

"Gee, why didn't *I* think of that?"

His fists clenched in his pockets, Griff issued a mental apology to Melinda's brother, who'd always seemed such an unreasonable tyrant when Griff and Melinda had been teenagers. Now Griff was rather surprised that Melinda hadn't spent her entire youth locked in her room. Perhaps if Matt, rather than her sister Merry, had been the twins' guardian, Melinda's fate would have been just that. At the moment, Griff couldn't have blamed Matt for yielding to temptation.

WITH ANY OTHER WOMAN dressed as Melinda was, Griff would have chosen a suitably casual restaurant so as not to make her uncomfortable. He made no such concessions for Melinda. They'd been seated in the rather dressy Italian restaurant for perhaps five minutes before he resignedly acknowledged to himself that being inappropriately dressed didn't faze this woman. He guessed she would have worn the same outfit had she known he'd choose this particular place. She'd never been one to care about conventions. Chose, instead, to defy those conventions whenever it amused her.

There'd been a time when he'd been the same way. Now he told himself that he'd learned to manipulate those conventions to his own advantage, using his conformity as a tool with which to accomplish his objectives.

After ordering her dinner, Melinda leaned against the table on her elbows, rested her chin on her crossed hands and looked limpidly at Griff. "Was there anything in particular that you wanted to discuss tonight? Or do we sit here and try to make casual date conversation, the way we did last time we had dinner together?"

He shook his head slowly. "You're still trying to irritate me, aren't you? Why is it that you seem to like me better when I'm on the verge of strangling you?"

Her smile was bright, genuinely amused—and it made his stomach muscles clench in reaction. "You really are very perceptive," she observed cheerfully. "Must come in handy in your line of work."

He reached across the table and tugged at one of her hands, clasping it lightly in his to emphasize his point as he looked steadily at her. "Melinda, why won't you stop needling me and just try to enjoy our evening together? Can't we just try for a pleasant dinner without quarreling?"

Her smile turned wistful. "We tried that last time, remember? It was very awkward, very uncomfortable. And it made me sad."

"Sad?" he repeated, surprised.

She nodded, not quite meeting his eyes. "I couldn't help remembering how easily we once talked, how often we agreed with each other. Even when we quarreled back then, you never tried to convince me that your opinions were the only valid ones. We simply agreed to disagree occasionally."

"Aren't you the one trying to inflict your opinions now?" he countered. "You've decided that my profession is a less than honorable one, that my clients are sleazy capitalists, that I'm hiding the real me behind a false image. You haven't given me a chance to demonstrate the validity of my work or the contentment I've found with the changes I've made in my life."

Biting her lower lip in a manner that made him want to kiss away the marks, Melinda looked guilty. "I have done that, haven't I?"

"Yes," he replied with a faint smile. "You have. So why don't we start over? Why can't we forget the past and see each other as two contemporary adults who just might enjoy each other's company if we gave it a chance?"

Her hand turned in his, fingers curling upward. "Will you answer something honestly?"

"I'll try." His agreement was rather wary.

"Two questions. One, are you really happy now with your life the way it is?"

He'd promised to answer honestly. He struggled with that answer for several long moments before saying guardedly, "I'm not unhappy."

Her face softened. "That's not the same thing."

"I'm aware of that. What was your other question?"

She took a deep breath. "If you'd met me for the first time that day in court, if you and I had never known each other before, would you still have asked me out?"

The struggle was longer this time, the answer more reluctant, but no less truthful. "Probably not."

"I'm not really your type."

That blasted honest face of hers so clearly showed all her emotions. He read the hurt she couldn't quite conceal and felt like a real jerk. *She* was the one who'd wanted honesty, wasn't she? "Dammit, Melinda, you think you'd have gone out with someone like me if it hadn't been for that past relationship?" he demanded aggressively.

"Well, well, look who's here," an intrusive male voice commented before Melinda could answer. Griff noted her relief before turning reluctantly to the man standing beside their table.

"Hello, Myers."

Doyle Myers, the one associate from the law firm who most resented Griff's influence with Wallace Dyson, glanced pointedly at the table where Melinda's hand still lay entwined with Griff's. "Having a nice evening, Taylor?"

Griff released Melinda's hand and put his own in his lap, fist clenching beneath the cover of the linen tablecloth. "Very nice. And you?"

"Things are looking up." Myers gave an oily shark smile and extended a hand to Melinda. "Doyle Myers, one of Taylor's associates."

Her answering handshake was just long enough to be civil. "Melinda James."

Myers tilted his head, dark eyes glittering. "The psychologist who testified in the Hawlsey case?"

Griff gritted his teeth, knowing full well that Myers already knew the answer to that question.

"Yes." Her voice was cool.

Chuckling heartily, Myers shook his finger at her. "You're not a very popular person with our boss at the moment, you know. You know our boss, don't you? Wallace Dyson. A very powerful man. Perhaps you know his daughter, Leslie. She's about your age and I'm sure you have some—" he glanced at Griff "—mutual friends."

"If you'll excuse us, Myers," Griff growled, "our dinners have arrived. I'll see you at the office on Monday."

"Dyson won't like it that you're seeing me, will he?" Melinda asked quietly when Myers had strutted away and their dinners lay before them.

Griff shrugged more casually than he felt. "He's never interfered with my personal life before." That wasn't strictly true, but he didn't want Melinda worrying about him.

Before she could speak again, he picked up his fork and tasted his dinner. "This is very good. I was hungry."

Taking the hint, she turned to her own plate. As if in unspoken cooperation with his earlier suggestion that they get to know each other better, Melinda made no effort to avoid controversial topics during dinner. Politics, foreign policy, local events—they touched on all those subjects and more during the next hour, and Griff was fascinated by the rather convoluted workings of her bright, somewhat eccentric mind.

He was aware that it wasn't particularly gentlemanly of him to make comparisons with his dates with other women—Leslie, for example—but it was difficult not to do so. He found it refreshing that he wasn't having to struggle with innocuous small talk, nor to guard his words for fear of offending his companion. Melinda made no such concessions to him, and he reacted in kind. He was a conservative Republican, she a liberal Democrat, he a fervent supporter of a hard-line foreign policy, she a full-fledged pacifist, he supported capital punishment, she was opposed to it.

They were in agreement on equal pay for equal work, better social programs for the handicapped, employer-funded child care and more money for education. As they'd once done in the past, they chose several times to agree to disagree on the more volatile political or ideological opinions, despite their natural inclinations to argue their own sides.

Griff thoroughly enjoyed the evening. And by the time dinner was finished, he wanted her more badly than before, if that were possible.

So what the hell was he going to do about it? he wondered grimly, walking at her side toward her apartment door. Was he ready to complicate his life by becoming involved with Melinda James? There was no doubt in his mind that such an involvement would definitely lead to complications. Melinda was the type of woman who would draw controversy like an ice-cream truck drew children.

"Well, it's been—" Melinda began at her door, after turning the key in the lock.

Griff reached past her and shoved the door open. "I'm coming in."

Following him inside with a gusty sigh, Melinda scowled. "Do you *ever* wait to be invited in?"

His smile was rueful. "Most places," he admitted.

"Just not mine."

His smile deepened. "I'd be waiting a long time, wouldn't I?"

Give me strength, Melinda mentally moaned, trying unsuccessfully to steel herself against that wicked smile. He smiled so rarely like this—full, unguarded, totally natural. And every time he did, her willpower congealed into quivering gelatin. He'd asked something. What was it? Oh, yes. She chose to ignore the question. "Want some coffee?"

"No." He took a step closer, sliding his glasses into the breast pocket of his jacket as he did so.

Eyeing him warily, she cleared her throat. "I have some white wine, I think."

"No, thanks." He loomed over her, making her have to fight the temptation to cravenly step backward.

"Milk?" she tried faintly.

He chuckled. "I don't think so." His hand slipped into her hair, cupping the side of her head.

"I—uh—thought we were going to get to know each other—as old friends," she managed, vividly aware of the heat and strength of him so close she could almost feel his breath expanding his broad chest.

He lowered his head until his lips just missed touching hers. "I've been wanting to do this all evening," he murmured. "It was all I could do to wait until we were alone."

Her hand lay on his chest, just over his thumping heart. "Griff, I—"

His mouth brushed hers, lifted only a fraction of an inch. "What?"

Her lips tingled wildly. What had she been going to say? "Oh, the hell with it." She locked both arms around his neck. "Are you going to kiss me or what?"

His laugh was smothered against her lips.

She'd wondered if that other kiss had been a fluke, wondered if any kiss could possibly be as powerful as she'd found that one to be. She'd almost convinced herself that tangled emotions and bittersweet memories had combined to add an unreal element to that first adult kiss between her and Griff. It couldn't possibly have been all that much different from any kiss she'd shared with any other man, she'd decided after a passage of hours.

She'd been wrong. No other man had ever affected her like this. No other man had ever curled her toes in her shoes, scattered her thoughts like multicolored bits of confetti, stirred her body into raging, aching need . . . with only a kiss. She couldn't analyze the difference at the moment—for that matter, she could hardly remember her name at the moment—but she gloried in that difference, her mouth opening to his welcome intrusion.

Griff pulled her close, his hands sweeping her back beneath the loose-fitting vest, the warmth of his palms penetrating the beige T-shirt. She crowded even closer, plucking ineffectively at his snugly tailored jacket. Didn't he ever feel strangled in those button-down establishment uniforms? she wondered hazily, tugging futilely at his severely knotted silk tie.

His hand had already found its way beneath her T-shirt to the smooth, rapidly overheating skin beneath. The loose waist of her baggy fatigue pants offered no resistance when his fingers slid inside to stroke the soft flesh at the hollow of her back. She managed to work two fingertips between the buttons of his crisp white shirt, finally feeling skin beneath. He was warm, solid. She wondered if his chest was smooth or hairy, tanned or pale. She wondered if she'd have to rip off buttons to find out.

"Melinda," he groaned into her mouth when she undulated eagerly against him. His hands clenched at her hips, holding her tightly against him, letting her feel what she did to him. "You could drive a man insane."

Even to her ears, her laugh was sultry. "I want to make you insane," she murmured, rising on tiptoe to trace his mouth with the tip of her tongue. "I want you wild and reckless and dangerous."

He frowned. "But I'm not—"

She planted her mouth hard on his, pulling up to him by her arms, which she'd locked again around his neck. She was delighted that he didn't even try to resist, but lifted her more securely against him, mumbling his pleasure as her tongue thrust boldly to explore the hot, moist depths of his mouth. And then they were sinking, dropping to their knees on the deep carpeting, mouths avid, hands insatiable, bodies straining, yearning toward a finale that was rapidly becoming inevitable.

Both hands buried deeply in her thick, tousled hair, Griff ravaged her mouth over and over, deeper and longer, until they breathed only in frantic, ragged gasps between kisses. He shifted, and she lay on her back, straining upward as his hands explored her from throat to knee, pausing to knead her throbbing breasts, smooth her quivering stomach, squeeze her inner thigh. Murmuring incoherently, he planted hot, biting kisses over her face and throat as he lowered her zipper and slid his hand beneath the tiny silk bikini panties she wore beneath the heavy trousers.

"Oh, yes," she whispered when his fingertips stroked the damp, dark secrets he discovered.

"You like that?" His voice was raw, hoarse, aroused.

"Oh, yes." Her eyes closed tightly as she arched upward. "Oh, Savage, it's so—"

He stiffened. And then she was alone, sprawled on the carpet as he shoved himself to his feet and turned away from her.

Blinking in disbelief at the abrupt return to sanity, she cleared her throat and tugged at her disheveled clothing, noting in distant incredulity that his tie was still neatly knotted. Must be one hell of a tight knot, she thought, even as she asked tentatively, "Griff? What's wrong?"

6

GRIFF'S DARK EYES were stormy when he turned his head to look at her, his body held stiffly, hands shoved deeply into his pockets. He couldn't have conveyed a clearer message of rejection had he worn a sign saying Hands Off, Melinda thought in bewilderment.

"What is it?" she asked again, pushing herself upright and shoving her hair away from her face.

"You called me Savage." The words were bitten out almost violently.

Watching him, she stood, straightening her clothes as she did so. "Did I? I didn't realize it."

"*You called me Savage!*"

She exhaled in exasperation at the furious repetition. "Okay, so I called you Savage. What's the big deal?"

He shook his head in obvious disbelief. "You don't even know."

"No! I don't know. So explain. Why are you so upset that I called you Savage? It's a nickname, left over from a friendship that meant a great deal to me at one time. It was hardly an insult."

"How many times do I have to tell you," he asked coldly, "that the boy you knew as Savage is gone? He no longer exists."

Growing as angry as he, Melinda planted her hands on her hips. "Then who the hell was that on the floor with me just now?"

His face darkened. "The name is Griff. I thought we'd reached a point where you knew that."

She threw both hands up in frustration, then tried to speak reasonably, as if to a borderline hysterical patient. "I'm aware that you prefer the name Griff. However, I knew you for nearly a year as Savage, and whenever I've thought of you during the twelve years since you left Springfield, it was by that name. It's not so unusual that I occasionally slip. If I'd started answering to *my* middle name since you knew me, you'd have a hard time remembering to call me Alice, wouldn't you?"

"Oh, hell, not that soothing, solicitous psychologist routine. That's really all I need right now."

"Dammit, Griff, what *do* you want me to say? I made a mistake, okay? I'm sorry. I'll try never to do it again. Would you like me to throw myself out a window now?"

"Well," he muttered, "at least that's a more honest response. I can deal with your temper a lot easier than with your psycho babble."

She dragged both hands through her hair. "This is crazy. I'm beginning to think *you're* crazy. Or maybe I am for trying to understand you in the first place."

"Maybe you're right." His tone was grim, his expression shuttered. "Maybe I was deluding myself to think that you could ever learn to accept me the way I am now. That you could learn to like the man I've become, rather than continue to try to turn me into some wild kid. What was it you said when I was kissing you? You wanted me wild and reckless and, uh . . ."

"Dangerous," she supplied irritably, cheeks warming at the memory of her behavior.

His lips curled. "Yeah. Well, I'm not any of those things, Melinda. I'm an average guy trying to make it in a world that rewards conformity. I decided a long time ago that I wanted to succeed in that world, and I've done pretty much whatever was necessary to make that happen. There are things I haven't done, things I won't do—I have my own code of ethics that is as important to me as yours is to you—but I'm somebody now and I'm not going to jeopardize that."

"Oh, Griff," she murmured sadly, wanting so badly to reach out to him. Knowing he'd reject her if she did. "You were always somebody. You were special. You belonged to no one but yourself, made no compromises, no concessions. There were a lot of things about your life that you hated, but you were always so self-assured. You liked yourself—and so did I."

Her sadness was mirrored in his dark eyes. "Are you never going to give yourself a chance to like me again?"

"How can I when you won't let me get close enough to know you? You've got yourself wrapped in so many socially acceptable layers that whatever real, honest emotions you have left are so deeply buried they may never surface again."

"And you're so hung up on an old memory that you can't accept reality. This *is* me, Melinda! You're looking at all there is to see."

She scanned expressively from his close-cut hair to his annoyingly neat tie, all the way down to his mirror-shiny leather shoes. "I can't believe that."

"You have no choice."

She took a step closer to him, reaching out to catch his arm in one urgent hand. "Griff, listen to me, please. It's not that I want to change you into something you're not, that I don't admire the man you've become. I do, very much. It's just that I don't think it's healthy for you to completely deny your past. You didn't suddenly come into existence two years ago when you joined Dyson's law firm. You're only going to make yourself miserable trying to live as if you did."

"Let me worry about my mental health, will you? I'm not looking for a therapist."

"I don't know what you want from me," she whispered, staring up at him, trying and failing to read his face. "You claim to want to forget the past, and yet you still want to see me. You don't particularly approve of me, of the way I live my life, of my political or social opinions, and yet you still want to see me. Why?"

His eyebrow rose expressively. "You can ask that after what happened between us?"

She didn't like the implication that what he wanted from her was sex. "I won't be used," she told him fiercely. "I won't be a temporary release valve or serve as one last fling before you tie yourself down to some comfortable, conforming corporate wife."

His face hardened. "Leave Leslie out of this. I told you I had no plans to marry her."

"I never mentioned Leslie's name," she pointed out, her throat inexplicably tight.

Releasing his breath in a hard gust, Griff half turned away, shoving a hand through his hair, ruffling it appealingly over his forehead. "Hell. Can't you just accept that I enjoy your company, that I'm attracted to you, that I want to be with you? Do you have to analyze everything I say or do, rationalize every move we make?"

"I guess I can only answer that by quoting you. That's the way I am. I can't change."

He looked at her, thoughtfully. "You and I—we're all wrong together, aren't we?"

"It would appear that way," she agreed unhappily, arms crossed in front of her.

"So why can't I stay away?"

She gave a half shrug, moistening her lips. "Why can't I ask you to?"

After digesting her quiet words for a moment, he managed a semblance of a smile. "So you want to try again? Another date? Maybe we can do something different next time. How about a movie?"

Melinda James had never been afraid of anything in her life—not that she'd admit, anyway. No stunt had ever been too outrageous, no relationship too risky, no challenge too perilous, no problem too formidable. And yet, strangely enough, she found herself afraid now of accepting a simple invitation.

Griff had claimed he wasn't dangerous. She knew better. He could hurt her in a way that she'd always skillfully avoided being hurt before.

"Melinda?" he asked when her silence had extended uncomfortably.

The sound that escaped her was half sigh, half rueful laugh. "I don't suppose you'd believe I'm suddenly becoming the cautious type?"

His smile deepened, understanding in his eyes. "I'd find it rather doubtful."

"Think we can agree on what movie to see?"

"I'll even let you choose," he offered magnanimously.

She took a deep breath. "All right. We'll give it another try."

"Don't look so worried, Melinda. We're only agreeing to another date," he admonished, beginning to relax. "Tomorrow night?"

"Pick me up at seven."

"You're on." He shifted his weight, looked around the apartment as if he'd forgotten something, then shrugged and reached into his jacket for his glasses. "Guess I'd better go. I'll see you tomorrow."

"All right." She stood well out of his way as he walked to the door, not certain she could handle touching him again, just then. Her body still throbbed in slow, frustrated arousal, unwilling to accept that there would be no conclusion to the lovemaking he'd so skillfully initiated.

He opened the door, started to step through it, then paused to look at her. "Good night, Melinda."

"Good night. And Griff?"

"Yes?"

"Don't wear a tie tomorrow, okay?"

He grimaced. "Couldn't resist that, could you? I won't wear a tie." The door closed behind him with a rather peevish snap.

As if she'd been holding herself erect with nothing more than sheer willpower, Melinda sagged bonelessly the moment she was alone, her head falling back, eyes closing, breath escaping in a long, weary gust. And she wondered for the first time in her twenty-six reckless, adventurous years if she'd taken on more than she could handle by accepting another date with Griffin Taylor.

"UP AGAINST THE WALL, TAYLOR. Legs spread, hands above your head."

"What'd I do this time?"

"Gonna play innocent, huh?"

"Hey, be careful! I'm not carrying anything. What's your problem?"

"Liquor store holdup over on Second Street. Clerk said the perp was a punk kid with long, stringy blond hair. Sound familiar, Taylor?"

"Look, it wasn't me, all right? I've been right here, playing pool with the guys. Ask 'em."

"Oh, yeah, sure. Like your buddies are reliable witnesses. Tell your story at the station, kid."

"You're cuffing me? Come on, man, give me a break."

"You'll get your break in the lineup. Get in the car, Taylor. Don't make me put you in."

"I'm going. I'm going."

Sirens echoed in his head along with the memory of snarled accusations and curt instructions. Griff stirred restlessly against the pillows, the dream replay of that long-ago episode leaving a bitter, angry taste in his mouth. He'd been cleared of that robbery, but it hadn't been the first time he'd been accused falsely, assumed guilty. Nor had it been the last. Edward Taylor, Sr. was the meanest drunk in the county, and his son had rightly earned a reputation as a fighter and a trouble-maker. Griff, or Savage, as he'd proudly insisted on being called then, had been so full of helpless anger and frustration after his mother abandoned him that he'd struck out at anyone and everyone who'd gotten in his way.

The dream voices faded into silence, but the sirens continued, the sound shrill, intrusive, persistent. Griff frowned and opened his eyes, blinking against the on-slaught of daylight. Not sirens. He turned his head as the sound came again. The telephone.

Reaching out, he pulled the receiver to his ear, rub-bing his other hand across his bleary eyes. "Yeah?"

"Griff? I'm sorry, did I wake you?"

"Leslie? What time is it?" He squinted at the clock, trying to read the blurred numerals.

"It's nine-thirty. You're usually up long before this. Late night?" she asked delicately.

"Yeah. You could say that." He'd spent most of the night pacing, trying to understand his convoluted feel-ings for Melinda James, futilely attempting to walk off the seething sexual energy left over from their abruptly interrupted lovemaking. Then he'd fallen into bed, only to be haunted by snatches of memories he'd thought forever buried. Had it been Melinda who'd resurrected those unwelcome bits of his past? Would he ever com-pletely rid himself of them as long as she was around as a reminder?

". . . and I know it's short notice, but Daddy wanted me to ask you."

The elegantly modulated voice in his ear brought him to attention. He was guiltily aware that he'd drifted off. "I'm sorry, Leslie. What did you ask?"

She laughed lightly. "Goodness, you are out of it this morning, aren't you?"

"Yeah," he replied apologetically. "Haven't had my coffee yet."

"I understand. I'm sure you were staring at briefs and depositions until dawn. You workaholic attorneys are all alike. Just like Dad."

Wincing, he sat up. "So what was it you wanted, Leslie?"

"Dinner," she repeated patiently. "Tonight. Daddy's entertaining a rather important client and he told me— I mean, he suggested that I invite you as a date. It will be good exposure for you, of course."

Any other time there would have been no question that he'd accept the invitation. As she'd said, a private dinner with the Dyson family and an important client would certainly be a major step upward in Griff's career. "I'm sorry, Leslie. I already have plans for this evening. If you'd only asked me sooner . . ."

"The dinner came up unexpectedly. I tried to call you last night, but you were out."

She'd left her number on his machine. Twice. He'd ignored it. "I got in pretty late," he prevaricated.

"You can't change your plans?"

Of course he could. He could simply dial Melinda's number and reschedule. They were only going to a movie, after all. Something they could do any time. And he could spend the evening with the Dysons . . . with Leslie. "No, I'm sorry, I can't."

"All right. Daddy will be disappointed—as I am, of course," she added hastily.

"I'm sorry," he repeated.

"Another time, then?"

"Sure. I'll give you a call." But he knew even as he hung up the phone that he wouldn't be calling her. Melinda was changing everything, dammit. He'd suspected all along that she would.

So why wasn't he fighting harder against the attraction he felt for her? And why was he looking forward to the evening with more anticipation than he'd felt for anything in a very long time?

Muttering a curse beneath his breath, he slid from the bed and headed for the bathroom.

"YOU'RE THE PSYCHOLOGIST. Do you think he's one of those multiple personality types? Like Sybil or the three faces of Eve?"

"Come on, Meaghan, stop fooling around. This isn't funny," Melinda complained, rubbing her dully aching temple as she held the telephone to her ear.

"Sorry. But you have to admit it sounds kind of strange. I mean, arguing with Savage about whether or not he still exists. Very weird."

Melinda sighed. "Of course he exists, Meaghan. Well, Griff exists, anyway. It's Savage who—oh, forget it."

"See? Even you think it's strange—and that *is* frightening."

"So you see what I mean, then? It can't be healthy for him to repress his past this way. Someday it's going to come out. It's inevitable, especially if he really does have a political career in mind. How will he handle it when he does? If he can't face up to it now, what will happen when he's forced to publicly acknowledge it? I'm worried about him, Meaghan."

"As a concerned psychologist? Or is this getting more personal for you?" Meaghan asked shrewdly. "Sounds to me like you're getting involved—deeply involved."

Melinda laughed without humor. "You know the funny thing? He thinks he's waging some sort of campaign to make me like him again. He has no idea how easy. . . ."

"How easy?" Megan prompted anxiously when Melinda's voice faded away.

"How easy it would be to fall in love with him," Melinda admitted quietly. She couldn't have spoken that frankly to anyone but Meaghan. There was no way she could have disguised her feelings with her twin.

"Oh, Melinda." It was a tone Melinda had heard many times before. The one that said, "You're heading for trouble again."

"I know," she answered with a sigh, as if those unspoken words had been uttered aloud. "We're totally wrong for each other. He wants someone sophisticated and conservative, someone who'll stand quietly in the background as a foil to his brilliant career. Someone who agrees with everything he says, doesn't embarrass him in public or private."

"If that's the type of woman he really wants, then why is he hanging around *you?*" Meaghan demanded tactlessly.

Wincing, Melinda shrugged. "Darned if I know."

"And let's face it, Melinda, he's not exactly the type you've favored in the past, either. I mean, a hard-nosed attorney? A defender of big corporations in personal injury cases? A *Republican?*"

Laughing reluctantly at her sister's exaggerated teasing, Melinda felt her headache beginning to ease, as she'd known it would when she'd dialed Meaghan's number. "I know, I know. Believe me, I know. It's ridiculous. And yet—"

"And yet?"

"He makes my teeth sweat."

"Button-down shirts and all?"

"I even think his silk ties are sexy," Melinda confessed almost sheepishly. She didn't add that there'd been at least one occasion when the silk tie had been very much in her way.

"Wow. Maybe you *are* in love."

"Mm. So what should I do about it?"

"Head for the hills," Meaghan said promptly.

"You're probably right."

"And you're going to stay right where you are."

"Yeah. I guess I am."

"Good luck, Melinda."

"Thanks, Meggie. I think I'm going to need all the luck I can get. I've got to go. Say hi to John and Andy for me. I guess John will think this is hysterically funny."

"No more than I do," Meaghan teased, then sobered. "Don't get hurt, Melinda."

"Hey, I never do, right?"

"You never have before," Meaghan corrected. "I've always worried that someday you would."

"Yeah," Melinda murmured, staring ahead with unfocused eyes. "So have I. Bye, Meaghan."

There was a sort of twisted irony in the situation, she thought after she'd cradled the telephone receiver. She'd always been so glib, so smug about love. Always danced just out of reach of that particular emotion, even as she'd laughed secretly at the foolishness of its victims. She'd heard her sisters cry during their courtships, worried through the inevitable, though mercifully brief, rocky times in their happy marriages. She'd seen her brother nearly brought to his knees when he and his then-future wife had broken up after a bitter quarrel. Matt, the strongest, most arrogantly self-assured man she'd ever known, had proven as vulnerable, as brittle as anyone when it came to love.

Even then, Melinda thought she was somehow immune to that kind of pain. All she had to do, she'd reasoned, was to remain in control. But that was before some twist of fate's warped sense of humor had brought Griffin Taylor into her life. She hadn't been quite in control since the moment their eyes had clashed in that courtroom. And she wasn't at all sure what she was going to do about it.

Focusing on the hot-pink and blue neon nostalgia clock on the wall ahead of her, she groaned and shoved herself off the couch. There wasn't time to worry about it now. Griff would be picking her up in less than an hour. That didn't give her much time to choose an outfit guaranteed to make him swallow his tongue, she thought with a renewed surge of characteristic mischief. There was that sexy little number in turquoise and fuchsia that she'd never quite had the nerve to wear before. But, for Griff . . .

She smiled wickedly.

"How could you be so nice to that man?" Melinda's voice echoed off the walls of the hallway as she stormed toward her apartment later that evening.

"Melinda, he's my client. I *have* to be nice to him. Besides, he's not so bad."

"Tell that to the six people who died in the fire in his building, all because the jerk was too cheap to install a sprinkler system."

"There is no proof that a sprinkler system would have saved those people. Even the fire marshall said that."

"He also said that a sprinkler system *might* have given them a chance. I'm sure they would have taken any chance they could get."

"Stanley is very sorry about what happened . . ."

She shoved her door key into the lock. "Oh, sure he is. And he's even sorrier that he's going to have to pay out a fortune in damages."

"That's up to a jury to decide."

"Right. Let's keep it in the courts as long as possible, wasting the court's time and the taxpayers' money so your client can continue to earn interest on all his ill-gotten gains!"

"So," Griff asked blandly, closing the door of her apartment behind them. "What do you think? It was a pretty successful date, don't you agree?"

Melinda stared at him in disbelief, mouth slightly open. They'd been quarreling since they left the restaurant where they stopped for dessert after the movie, since Stanley Schulz had stopped by their table for a jovial little chat with Griff while Melinda glowered silently in her seat. He called that a successful date? "You don't get out much, do you?"

He chuckled. "Enough."

She looked from him to the door, planting her hands on her hips with a grimace of resignation. "You've done it again, haven't you? Waltzed right in here without an invitation."

"Want me to leave?" he offered politely.

She sighed. "You're already in. You might as well stay for a while."

Grinning, he tossed his poplin jacket over the back of a chair. "That's the most gracious invitation I've had in weeks. How could I refuse?"

Narrowing her eyes, she stepped closer to him and reached up to trace a fingertip along the bridge of his nose. "Amazing," she murmured as if to herself.

Watching her in wary amusement, he asked, "What?"

"Your nose has never been broken, has it?"

"No."

She stepped back, shaking her head. "You must be very quick. Because I'm absolutely positive that there've been plenty of people who've taken swings at it over the years. You, Griffin Taylor, can be a very annoying man."

Laughing, he tweaked her chin. "So I've been told."

"I was furious with you a minute ago. I'm sure I was," she muttered, glaring at him in frustration. "Weren't we just having a fight?"

He rounded his eyes in faked surprise. "Of course we weren't fighting. We were simply disagreeing over an aspect of my job. We knew we would occasionally."

"You were mad at me, too. Admit it."

He made a face and nodded. "Well, yeah. But I decided to let it go. We've got better things to do than spend the rest of the evening arguing about one of my clients."

"But, Griff, this is important. It's what you do. How do you expect me to . . ." She paused as his words sank in. "What better things?"

His smile gave her his answer. Her heart stopped, then resumed at double speed. "How about some coffee?" she asked quickly, her voice sounding entirely too squeaky for her satisfaction.

His laugh was husky, very male, and oh, so sexy. "I don't want coffee. And I don't want wine or even milk. I want you, Melinda. I've wanted you from the first moment I saw you again."

Her knees dissolved. "Oh, Griff, I want you, too," she whispered, unable to be anything but completely honest at this crucial moment. No matter how dangerous that honesty may be.

"Then what are you doing way over there?" he asked encouragingly, holding out his arms.

She flew into them, face lifting for his kiss. His mouth covered hers, his tongue thrusting inside without preliminaries. She reacted with urgent, fiery, rapacious hunger. Hauling her closer, Griff made it clear that he exulted in her passionate response.

She murmured her satisfaction when her hands found their way beneath the snug white knit polo shirt he'd worn with navy poplin slacks. Conservative, perhaps, but so much more accessible than his severely tailored suits, she thought happily, stroking the warm, sleek skin of his back, tracing his spine from nape to waist.

"Did I remember to tell you how gorgeous you look tonight?" Griff murmured, lifting his head to look at her admiringly, his hands busily reacquainting themselves with her willing curves.

"I think so." She smiled as she remembered the moment she'd opened her door to him earlier that evening. He'd taken one look at her brief, brightly colored dress and choked. He'd rushed her to his car, barely giving her time to grab her purse or lock the door. All in all, she'd been quite satisfied with that response. Just as she was with the look in his eyes now.

"You're gorgeous." He touched his mouth to hers. "You're beautiful." He brushed her lips again. "You're exquisite."

She caught his face between her hands and pressed her mouth to his. "Don't tell me," she whispered, pulling away just far enough to allow her lips to shape the words. "Show me."

"I was hoping you'd say that." Smiling piratically, he lifted her against his chest and headed for the bedroom.

Her dress quickly made a colorful puddle on the carpet beside the bed, his slacks and shirt a more sober pile nearby. Scraps of lace so sheer as to be almost unnecessary floated down to join them as Griff's hands swept Melinda's eager body, divesting her of the last scraps of fabric hiding her from him.

"Beautiful," he murmured against her breast, one long, hard leg tangling with her softer ones. "So damned beautiful."

She forced her heavy lids to remain open, not wanting to miss a moment of his lovemaking. His body was as perfect as she'd imagined it would be—strong, fit, tanned. His chest was smooth, almost hairless, the muscles splendidly defined. She'd never seen a more beautiful man, and she delighted in telling him so.

He hesitated only long enough to ascertain that she was protected, then he proceeded to drive her to madness. He explored so thoroughly that there was no inch of her that escaped his slow, skillful ministrations. She was wild by the time he made his way back to her mouth. Arching, gasping, needing as she'd never needed before. Incapable of saying even his name, she urged him on with ardent hands, letting him know how desperately she wanted him. A strangled cry escaped her when he thrust inside, stretching her, filling her, driving her even higher. The feelings were new, shattering, and yet somehow familiar. As if she'd always known this was waiting for her. As if she'd somehow saved a part of herself for him alone.

Love. She'd always danced around it. Now she threw herself wholeheartedly into its embrace.

And when her body convulsed with a climax that bordered the boundaries of consciousness, when Griff gasped and shuddered within her arms, she was dimly aware that she would never be the same. She couldn't be hurt before because she'd never made herself vulnerable. Griff had stripped away all her defenses, all her bravado, all her bold camouflage as easily as he'd rid her of her colorful clothing. And for the first time, she knew what true vulnerability meant.

She'd always recognized the danger in him, from the time he'd been a boy. Now she realized that the danger had always been to her own heart.

"I KNOW I SHOULD TELL HIM I never want to see him again, but I just can't stand the thought of being alone. I mean, isn't a jerk better than no man at all?"

"No, Twyla," Melinda told her patient gently. "These destructive relationships you keep getting into are only going to get you hurt—seriously hurt, if you're not careful. You have to learn that you can be happy on your own, that you're strong enough, bright enough to make a life for yourself without a man until someone comes along who is right for you."

"That's easy for you to say." Twyla's full lower lip extended in a near pout. "You're thin and gorgeous and smart. You've got this job that pays good and gets you lots of respect. You don't have any trouble getting great guys to notice you. Look at me. I don't have any of that stuff."

Melinda sighed, brushing her hair away from her face with a somewhat heavy hand. It was late in the afternoon of a long, mind-wearying day. Unfortunately, she was having a very hard time keeping her thoughts away from her own problems.

"Twyla, you have a great deal to offer. We've been through this, remember. You don't have to be a victim. Jim is using you—he's abusing you. And he'll continue to do so for as long as you let him."

Twyla's heavily accented eyes were resentful, mirroring her reluctance to admit her own fault in her present despondency. "I bet you've got someone, don't you?"

"It won't do you any good to waste the last few minutes of our hour discussing my personal life, will it?"

"Yeah, but you do, don't you? You've got somebody."

Melinda caught herself toying restlessly with one oversize zebrawood earring. Then she pulled her hand away, resting it in her lap. "I'm seeing someone," she admitted. Seeing someone? *Ha!* She was raving crazy dancing in the street in love with that someone, and at the moment, she couldn't have said if she had any better chance of success with that relationship than Twyla had with the obnoxious Jim.

And *she* was supposed to be giving advice?

"You're here to talk about your problems, Twyla."

Twyla nodded as if to emphasize her point and murmured miserably, "I don't want to be alone, Ms. James."

Melinda sighed. She and Twyla had a long way to go.

Glancing at her gaudy, rhinestone-studded watch, Twyla shoved herself out of the worn blue chair beside Melinda's desk. "I gotta go or I'll be late to work. If I'm late again, I'm going to get canned."

Twyla was a waitress at an unsavory bar in a section of town that was safe only for rats and roaches at night. Melinda couldn't stand the thought of the unhappy young woman working there night after night—particularly since she knew most of the money Twyla made was being used for liquor and heaven knew what else for her abusive lover. But there was only so much she could accomplish all at once. Her job now was simply to help the woman develop self-esteem. Only then could Twyla realize that she didn't need to subjugate herself to any man who'd pay a bit of attention to her.

"Be careful, Twyla."

The other woman shrugged. "Does it really matter?"

"It matters to me."

Twyla hesitated, as if testing the words for sincerity, then managed a somewhat shy smile. "Thanks, Ms. James. I'll be back next week, okay?"

"All right. In the meantime, think about what we discussed today, will you?"

"I will. I promise."

Melinda waited until the office door had closed behind the woman before crossing her arms on her desk and hiding her face in the crook of her elbow. She felt as though she were butting her head against a wall with Twyla. The woman's sense of self-worth was nil; for Twyla, it took a man to give her an identity. She threw herself from one bad relationship to another, needing only an invitation, no matter how careless, to become involved.

In contrast, Melinda had always carefully guarded her independence, resulting in involvement in only a very select few relationships, none of which had provided what she'd wanted for the long term. And yet now both Twyla and Melinda were caught up in affairs that seemed destined to end in heartbreak.

Not that Melinda and Griff were having an affair, exactly. One night hardly constituted an affair. For that matter, it didn't even count as one full night; Griff had left sometime after midnight, claiming he had to be up early the next morning.

She'd been too dazed, exhausted and lovestruck to ask why he'd have to be up early on a Sunday morning. She hadn't had the chance to ask him since—because she hadn't heard from him since. He'd made love to her twice, left her in the wee hours of the morning, and hadn't so much as called her. And it was now Wednesday.

She really didn't appreciate being treated as a one-night stand, she told herself. She should be furious with him for such callous behavior. And she would be—if she didn't so completely understand it.

Griff had been as awed by their lovemaking as she had been. He hadn't been able to hide his emotions from her, any more than she had from him. What they'd found together had been something momentous, and neither of them knew what, exactly, to do about it.

She was in love with him. She wasn't quite confident enough to believe that Griff felt the same way. If he did love her, she wasn't sure he'd admit it to her or to himself. But she'd gotten to him. Close enough to make him bolt in panic. He'd found himself falling for someone who wasn't at all the type of woman he'd decided was right for him, someone who reminded him all too clearly of a past he'd worked so hard to forget. And he'd run.

Should she call him? Should she give him time to work out his feelings? What if he succeeded in repressing those feelings? What if he convinced himself that their relationship would never work? What if he decided never to see her again?

What if she went into his office and threw herself at his feet, begging him to give them a chance?

"Oh, my God," she groaned into her arms, appalled at her uncharacteristic indecision, her atypical lack of pride where Griff was concerned. "What's happening to me?"

"Face it, James. You're losing it."

The cheerful observation brought her head up with a jerk. "Fred! Dammit, you scared me out of my shoes. What do you want?"

He grinned at her, draped over the couch as if he'd been there all day. "Oh, nothing. I've just been sitting here enjoying the spectacle of Melinda James falling apart."

Scowling at him, she tossed her head. "You're a psychologist, remember? You're supposed to help people in this condition, not make fun of them."

"You're right. Want to talk about it?"

"No."

He made a gesture of resignation with one hand. "So much for help. Looks like making fun is all I can do for you."

"Do me a favor. Don't do me any favors."

"Aren't you in a lovely mood," he commented facetiously. "Some might even call it a *savage* mood."

She lifted her lip in a near snarl. "I'm warning you, Fred."

"Does he know you're in love with him?"

After a long, taut pause, Melinda cleared her throat. "Psychologists," she grumbled. "I had to work with psychologists. They're not content to tinker with other people's minds, they have to read them, as well."

"So you are in love with him?"

"It's . . . possible," she admitted reluctantly.

"How possible?" he persisted.

"Very possible. Highly possible. Extremely possible."

"And how does he feel?"

"Like heading for the hills," Melinda replied flatly, remembering Meaghan's advice to her. Advice she should have taken, she thought dispiritedly. Maybe if she had, she wouldn't be hurting like this.

"I can understand that," Fred mused. "If I found myself on the verge of getting deeply involved with Melinda James, I'd probably have an urge to run for cover."

"Oh, thanks so much. With friends like you . . ."

He grinned. "Don't mention it. Besides, I'm sure he'll realize eventually that he's only resisting the inevitable. He'll come around. He just needs time to get used to the idea."

Her chin lifted. "I don't know that I *want* him to come around," she muttered. "I'm getting tired of his advance and retreat games. *He's* the one who insisted on going out with me. He's the one who—well, anyway, it isn't as if I've been chasing him."

"Yeah, but you're not the one who's been trying to play let's pretend for the past few years, either," Fred pointed out. "Griff's got a lot of things to work out, Melinda. From what you've said, he's still a long way from coming to terms with his past. There's a lot of unresolved anger floating around in that young-executive body, and if you're not careful, it's all going to blow up in your direction."

"I know. Believe me, I know. If he were coming to me for counseling, I'd know what to do. I'd make him face up to that past, encourage him to share his feelings, suggest that he's repressing too much, that he's in danger of a severe emotional blow when he can no longer hold it inside. But I can't be objective with this one, Fred. I can't hurt him by making him remember things he's more comfortable forgetting. I can't risk messing up this lucrative, influential position he has. From everything I hear, Wallace Dyson holds absolute power in his firm. Anyone who displeases him will find himself on a fast track to anonymity. I don't want that to happen to Griff because of me."

"You're so sure it would happen if you get involved with him?"

"I know Dyson's furious with me for testifying on Nancy's behalf. I know that he has an eye on Griff as a potential son-in-law. I know that I'll never be able to stand meekly back and hold my opinions to myself when Griff defends clients I think are blatantly in the wrong. Does that sound like I'll be an asset to his career?"

"Well . . ."

"And Griff knows all that as well as I do. I'm sure that's part of what's bothering him—one of the drawbacks he's considering before calling me. I don't want to hurt him, Fred. I don't want to be a handicap for him. And yet . . ."

"And yet . . . ?"

She pounded her fists impotently against the desktop. "He's not *happy!* He's living a masquerade, worried that someone will want to know too much about his past, concerned that he'll somehow mess up and end up on the streets again. He can't believe that he deserves every good thing that has happened to him because of his hard work and determination. He thinks he's made it because no one really knows the truth about him. He was actually considering marrying Leslie Dyson just to advance his career. I'm sure he was, despite his denials. For all I know, he's still considering it."

She took a deep, shaky breath and tried to calm down. Looking into Fred's sympathetic eyes, she said more quietly, "I asked him if he was happy with his life and the most he could say was that he wasn't unhappy. I told him that wasn't the same, and he agreed. I can't stand to think of him living that way."

"You think *you* can make him happy?"

"I don't know," she whispered. "I only know I want to try. But what if I just mess everything up? What if I ruin everything and then he really is unhappy. Maybe I should just get out of his life and let him find his own answers."

"And maybe you should hang in there and fight for what you want," Fred countered. "For what you believe is right for both of you."

She dragged a hand through her disheveled hair. "It sounds so easy, doesn't it? We sit here day after day and tell people what they should do. And when it comes right down to it, no one really knows what the answers are."

"'No one who, like me, conjures up the most evil of those half-tamed demons that inhabit the human breast, and seeks to wrestle with them, can expect to come through the struggle unscathed,'" Fred quoted cheerfully.

Melinda dropped her hand and stared at him in disbelief. "Freud? *You're* quoting Freud?"

"I've read him. I almost never agree with him, but I have read him."

"What does that have to do with anything, anyway?"

"It means, my dear, confused partner, that we poor headshrinkers are no more immune to the batterings of human emotions than any other poor mortal. It's always easier to sit back and give objective advice when you have nothing personal at stake. But when it's our own heart or our own future, then everything's different. If there were any perfect, finite answers, then there wouldn't be so many different schools of thought in the mental health field, now would there?"

"Okay," she dared him, "you're an objective observer. Tell me what I should do."

He stood with an indulgent smile. "Wrong. I'm not at all objective. My first impulse is to track Griffin Taylor down and punch him in the teeth for upsetting you. The only reason I haven't is because he's bigger than I am."

Reluctantly amused, Melinda laughed. "I'm going home. Maybe I'll find the answers between the covers of a book."

"Going to read psychology manuals?"

"No," she replied lightly, "romance novels. Good night, Fred."

"'Night, Melinda."

She stopped to kiss his cheek on the way out the door. "Thanks for making me talk—and for listening."

"Anytime, kid. You'll get my bill next week."

"Jerk," she muttered, but she was smiling when she left.

BREATHING SUSPENDED, heart thudding painfully, he watched her coming down the hallway. Her gleaming, strawberry blond head was lowered as she dug in a huge leather shoulder bag for her keys. She wore oversize wooden jewelry with a rakish khaki top and a jungle-print skirt. Heeled leather boots concealed her legs, but he knew exactly how slender and shapely they were. How strong they'd felt wrapped around his hips as he'd driven himself into her. He'd felt chained to her then, wondered if he'd ever be free of her. And he'd wanted to freeze time, just to make sure he wouldn't be.

She drew closer, muttering irritably when the keys eluded her. In his head, he heard the echoes of her passion—her voice, husky and breathless, crying his name, gasping her pleasure. His body hardened in warm remembrance and hopeful anticipation.

Three days stretched behind him. Long, tormented days of wanting her, endless hours of soul-searching, wondering if his need for her would break him in the end. Coming to the conclusion that it no longer mattered. It was too late. She'd taken him into herself and, in doing so, had seized a part of him that he had no hope of regaining. And even if she destroyed him in the end, he could never regret having captured a shooting star in his eager hands, no matter how briefly.

He heard the rattle of metal against metal as her fingers closed over the keys in the bag. Any moment she would look up and see him leaning against the wall beside her door. Would she welcome him? Would there be fury, even hurt, that he'd waited so long? Had she, perhaps, come to her own conclusions during the past three days? Decided that the leather-jacket-and-earrings version of him was more attractive than the establishment attorney he'd become? Did she still long for the rebel, reject the conformist? Could anyone hope to hold a shooting star?

Their eyes met. Hers widened and her step faltered. For what seemed an eternity, her face was void of expression, though her cheeks seemed to have lost color, her eyes blazing emerald in the pale oval of her face. His chest ached dully. He wondered if it was because he hadn't taken a complete breath since she'd stepped into the hallway... or because his heart was breaking at the rejection he feared.

And then she smiled, and his heart cracked at the sheer beauty of it. "Hi, Griff," she murmured, reaching out to him. "It's good to see you."

He took her hand in his, and accepted his fate.

THE ROOM WAS FILLED with the sweet scent of vanilla from the dozens of white candles that made shadows dance in the darkest corners. The seductive whisper of silk against skin could just be heard above the ragged breathing and quiet moans of the nude man lying on his back in the center of the large bed. His glistening chest rose and fell in the flickering candlelight, his tautly drawn face pulled into a grimace of pleasure that bordered on pain.

Wearing nothing but a lacy black teddy that did little more than highlight her most feminine attributes, Melinda sat astride Griff's rock-hard thighs, her hair tumbled around her shoulders, her hands sweeping his quivering body. She had warned him that she intended to punish him for staying away so long without a call; he was enjoying every moment of the torture she inflicted on him.

Bending over him, she allowed her hair to fall around them as she pressed her open mouth to the base of his throat. The skin was soft there—one of the few soft places she'd found on his firm, solid body. Trailing wet, nipping kisses from his throat to one hardened brown nipple, she stroked another of those intriguingly soft spots, the vulnerable hollow where groin blended into thigh. He squirmed restlessly as her fingers brushed tantalizingly close to a part of him that wasn't at all soft—not at the moment, anyway. Her hand closed over him at the same time her teeth sank delicately into his chest.

Griff gasped and arched upward as if electrified. "God, Melinda," he groaned hoarsely. "You're killing me."

Her husky laugh was nothing short of wicked. "You're not going to die, Griff. You're only going to think you have before I'm finished."

Growling impatiently, he reached for her, but she eluded him, catching his wrists and pinning them to the pillow above his head. "No," she said firmly, "You owe me this, Griffin Taylor, for putting me through three days of worry. I hate worrying."

"I just went through three damned miserable days, myself," he pointed out.

She leaned over to catch his earlobe between her teeth. Releasing it, she murmured, "And whose fault was that?"

"Yours."

She laughed again and covered his mouth with hers, bringing the conversation to an end.

He made no further attempt to control the lovemaking, abandoning himself to her skillful hands. There was no part of him that those hands missed. Minutes? Hours? Days? He neither knew nor cared how much time passed.

Through love-dazed eyes he watched as she tossed her hair back and lowered one thin strap of her teddy, her gaze locked with his. And then the other strap fell and the teddy slithered downward, revealing her small, beautifully molded breasts, their rose tips peaked as if in invitation. He covered them and then drew her slowly down to his hungry mouth. The teddy melted away as he feasted eagerly on the sweet taste of her. Glazed with passion, they hugged each other fiercely, heightening the sensation of closeness, the illusion of oneness.

As frenzied as he was, Melinda moved feverishly, rising to take him into her in one strong, sure thrust. His fingers digging into her hips, he arched to embed himself more deeply.

Neither could have said who set the rhythm of their loving, who controlled the speed, the depth of the strokes that carried them higher and higher. Ragged breathing synchronized to the movements of their bodies, they arched in perfect unison. And when the explosion came, it took them simultaneously, hurtling both beyond thought, beyond sanity, beyond the boundaries of mortal flesh. It would be much later before either recovered sufficiently to realize the full extent of the miracle they'd shared, the shattering climax neither had ever, could ever know with any other lover.

Limp, damp, still joined, they sprawled bonelessly, gasping for breath. Eyes closed, they clung to the only reality left in the aftermath of insanity—each other. And when they surrendered at almost the same moment to exhaustion, their names were little more than two broken whispers.

"Melinda."

"Griff."

And then they fell asleep.

8

IT HAD BEEN A WHILE since Griff had said his prayers. He was beginning to regret that, considering the close calls he'd encountered riding in the car being driven by Melinda James. Well *she* called it driving. He would have called it something altogether different. He was almost relieved he'd decided to leave his glasses at home that day. Some things shouldn't be seen too clearly. Things like—

"That truck, Melinda!" he warned, hands digging into the console of the tiny sports car she adored. He stared in horror at the rickety, produce-laden pickup weaving down the road ahead of them. The driver was obviously drunk. Almost as dangerous as Melinda.

"It's okay, Griff," she promised, turning to look reassuringly at him. "I see it." And then she smiled, speed never decreasing as she continued to look at her passenger.

"Melinda, watch out for the—" His breath hissed inward when she sped past the other vehicle with inches to spare. The breath came out on a sibilant expletive.

Melinda only laughed at him. "Honestly, Griff, you ride like someone's grandmother. Don't tell me you're one of those men who doesn't like to be driven by anyone but himself."

"I'm one of those men who doesn't like to be driven by maniacs," he replied grimly, seriously considering wrestling the wheel from her and hijacking the car. "Quit looking at me, dammit. Watch the road."

She sighed exaggeratedly. "Yes, Griff." Obediently, she turned her face forward, though he noticed no appreciable improvement in her driving.

"Where are we going, anyway?" he asked, keeping a cautious eye out for more threats to his life. She'd picked him up early this Saturday morning after assuring him that she was going to show him the time of his life. He'd accepted her invitation with some misgiving, aware of the perils involved in placing himself in Melinda's hands. Not that he'd known about her driving, of course, or he would have insisted on taking his car.

"I'm not sure." She didn't sound particularly concerned about it. "I'll know when we get there."

Griff could only sit back, white-knuckled, and hope the revelation would come soon.

Ten minutes later, Melinda gave an exclamation of delight as she spotted a skating rink and turned into a crowded parking lot with neck-whipping abruptness. "This is it!" she announced. "This is what I want to do this morning."

"No."

She turned beseeching, uptilted green eyes full force on him. "Come on, Griff, it'll be fun."

"No. Absolutely not."

"But, Griff, you used to be wonderful on roller skates. Remember how many times we—"

"Melinda, I'm thirty years old and I haven't been on skates in over twelve years. I'm not going to go in there now and make a fool of myself—not to mention that I'd be risking serious injury."

"Honestly, you've gotten so stuffy," she scolded. "Please, Griff."

He glared at her. "You're doing it again, aren't you? You're trying to change me into something I'm not any more. Trying to relive the past."

She rolled her eyes in obvious disgust. "I am *not* trying to relive the past. Do you honestly think I'd want to be fourteen again? And do you honestly think I'd want to go back to that sweet, platonic, hand-holding relationship with you now that I've discovered what a truly talented adult you've become?"

He was annoyed to feel his cheeks warm. "Melinda."

One hand clutching his arm, she gave him a smile that nearly melted him into the worn vinyl seat beneath him. "Griff, I still skate every chance I get. I love it. Particularly on family days," she added, glancing at the marquee. "The kids are so cute. Won't you just try it this once? For me?"

"Oh, hell."

Taking his words as a reluctant surrender, she flashed a big smile at him and leaned forward to kiss him. "Thank you," she murmured against his lips.

"You'll pay," he warned her, reaching for the door handle.

Her smile turned devilish. "I'm looking forward to it."

Clearing his throat violently, he stood for a moment beside the car, taking a few deep breaths of cool, early-autumn air so that he could regain enough composure to enter the family-oriented establishment. His neatly creased jeans hadn't felt quite so snug when he'd put them on earlier with his favorite white cotton sweater.

It didn't help to walk behind Melinda toward the door. Her near-white faded jeans molded tightly to her perfectly shaped bottom. Her turquoise and black geometric print top fit equally snugly; the first thing he'd noticed when she'd picked him up was how lovingly the fabric had clung to her breasts, making him itch to do the same. She smiled over her shoulder at him, oversize turquoise earrings brushing her soft cheeks, and he went weak at the knees. She expected him to *skate* in this condition? He'd probably break every bone in his body.

They'd spent nearly every day of the past three weeks together, whenever they weren't working, and he still found her the most fascinating woman he'd ever known. Outrageous, yes. Uninhibited, yes. Reckless, yes. Exasperating, yes. But still fascinating. He couldn't imagine ever being bored around her—and boredom had become so much a part of his life during the past few years that its absence was exhilarating. Not to mention the incredible upswing in his love life lately.

Griff paid for their admission, selected a battered pair of rental skates and sat beside Melinda on a carpet-covered bench to put them on. He watched as she kicked off her high-topped pink and white leather tennis shoes to reveal black and turquoise striped socks. He thought even the socks were sexy.

Her eyes laughing at him, Melinda nodded toward his skates. "Stop watching me and put them on. You don't really think I'm going to let you back out now, do you?"

He sighed and slipped off his soft leather Topsiders, wondering as he laced the first skate if there was some significance in their individual choices of footwear. And then he told himself he'd been spending too much time with a psychologist. Not that he intended to stop anytime in the near future, he thought with a faint smile.

Melinda was already on her feet, almost quivering with impatience to be on the impossibly crowded skating rink. "Ready?"

He took a deep breath and stood very slowly. Okay, so he could still stand up. On a carpeted surface. Now all he had to do was move. "Melinda, maybe we should—"

"Oh, no." She took his arm in a firm grip. "You promised."

He felt a muscle jump in his cheek and made a deliberate effort to relax. "I can't believe I'm doing this," he muttered. "I can't believe I let you talk me into it."

Laughing, she kept up easily with his somewhat awkward progress toward the hypnotically revolving skaters. "If it makes you feel any better, you're giving every teenage girl in the place palpitations. You really are a gorgeous man, Griffin Taylor."

"Oh, yes, that makes me feel much better." He almost snorted, cheeks warming again as his gaze collided with a staring fourteen-year-old redhead's. Her brightly painted eyes widened, then she looked away, collapsing in giggles into a group of friends. He felt more conspicuous than ever. "Dammit, Melinda."

She reached up to pat his cheek. "Don't feel so bad. I just had my bottom pinched by a twelve-year-old kid with a brush haircut and a bomber jacket."

"Great. We can both spend the next hour being ogled by juvenile delinquents. Boy, is this some fun."

"Fuddy-duddy." She glided onto the floor without a moment's hesitation. "Come on, Griff."

He waited for a lull in the circling crowd. Not finding one, he took his courage in his hands and stepped onto the smooth floor. Only to have his skate shoot right out from under him. He landed with a thud on his backside. Melinda doubled over laughing. "Yeah," he muttered, rising carefully, resisting the urge to rub his smarting posterior. "Some fun."

He managed three complete revolutions without falling again, though the first turn was a bit shaky.

"It's coming back to you, isn't it?" Melinda encouraged, skating effortlessly backward in front of him.

It was, actually—the roar of wheels, the squeals of laughter, the pounding rock music, the daring boys darting around the more hesitant skaters. Griff smiled as the memories assailed him. Melinda at fourteen, wearing miniskirted skating dresses over ruffled skating panties, dancing over the old wooden skating floor at the Four-Wheel Family Rink. Himself in leather and torn denim, shoulder-length hair flying around his face as he showed off with a spin, dangling silver earrings jingling with his movements—finishing the spin to bask in the applause of the swaggering toughs that made up his small circle of friends, guys who deigned to hang out at the skating rink only because the babes seemed to enjoy it. *Hey, yo, Savage. Lookin' good, man.*

Savage.

He stumbled, then recovered quickly, his smile fading to a frown. What was Melinda doing to him? He hadn't allowed memories like that to escape their mental coffin in years. Even the good memories were too dangerous, leading to the inevitable recollections of the hell he'd endured when he went home to a drunken father with a ready fist.

"Griff, what's wrong?" Turning to skate at his side, Melinda took his arm, looking up in concern. "You didn't hurt yourself when you fell, did you?"

"No, I'm fine." His voice must have sounded sincere, because her look of concern immediately faded. He was about to suggest that they leave when the rock song ended and the lights dimmed. As the silver ball overhead began to sparkle with multicolored lights, the deejay's voice announced a ladies' choice couples-only segment.

Melinda smiled at Griff and held out her hands to him. "You always were my choice," she murmured huskily.

Mesmerized by her smile, he took her hands in his.

The song was an old one by Boz Scaggs. The smooth, crooning voice filled the rink, underscored by the whirring of wheels. Teenagers held hands with their steadies, heads close together, the better skaters in classic dancing position, guys skating backward. Little girls skated with their daddies, little boys with their mommies, chubby legs pumping earnestly as they clung with total trust to steady, loving hands. A man and woman who had to be in their late sixties glided slowly just ahead, hands joined, skates synchronized from many years of practice.

"Love, what have you done to me?" Boz Scaggs asked in the song. His hands intertwined with Melinda's, eyes locked with hers, heart in his throat, Griff wondered the same thing.

The song faded. Melinda and Griff rolled to a stop. And then he kissed her, oblivious to the brightened lights and renewed noise around them.

They skated for another hour, until Griff's legs were aching from the unfamiliar activity, his ankles beginning to wobble a bit on the turns. He'd allowed Melinda to persuade him to try a few more daring moves, had found himself taking pride at skating backward again. It was a lot like riding a bike, he decided. It was all coming back to him.

And then a six-year-old demon with orange hair and a demented grin dashed right in front of him. Desperately trying not to fall on that kid or the two little girls skating close beside him, Griff fell hard—only to have the boy land flat on top of him. Griff's breath left his chest at the same moment a flailing skate caught him directly between the legs.

It was with almost superhuman effort that he refrained from clutching himself in agony. Nausea threatened; he forced it back. Supremely aware of the young eyes trained on him in concern, he gritted his teeth and assured the apologetic boy that he was fine. Just fine.

"Griff, are you all right?" Melinda knelt beside him, anxiously studying his face, which he knew must be rather pale.

Wiping the sheen of sweat from his upper lip, he rose painfully with her help. "I'm fine. Just fine," he snapped. "Let's get out of here."

Aware that his walk was a bit stiff-legged, he managed to get out of his skates and to Melinda's car without a word. Melinda hovered beside him. "Are you sure you're all right? You look a little green."

Without mincing words, Griff told her exactly where he was hurt.

Covering her mouth with one hand, she winced. "Oh, no. You're not—uh—"

"Permanently damaged? No." He rested his hand on the top of her undersize car as she hastily unlocked the door. "I just want to go home and sit down with a drink. And I would like to get home in one piece," he added vehemently, narrowing his eyes in warning.

"Would you like to drive?"

Exasperated with her obtuseness, he levered himself very carefully into the low passenger seat. "*You* are going to drive," he told her. "And you are going to drive as carefully as an elderly grandmother with a car full of babies, is that clear?"

"Yes, Griff," she replied meekly. It infuriated him that her voice was bubbling with the laughter she had too much sense to release.

Melinda couldn't have driven more carefully if he'd been a driving instructor and she a student taking her final exam. Which only led him to wonder if her earlier exhibition had been a deliberate effort to watch him sweat. "You," he told her when she pulled sedately into a parking space at her apartment building, "are dangerous."

"Why, Griff, my driving was exemplary," she answered in feigned innocence.

"Extremely dangerous," he added grimly.

Her smile faded, her eyes growing watchful. "Does that mean you want to run while you're still relatively unscathed?" she asked with an unsuccessful attempt at levity.

He studied her gravely. "Is that what this morning has been? A test to see if I can handle you in your most reckless moods? If I'm easily scared off?"

"Of course not," she denied immediately, heatedly. "I haven't been testing you." She paused a moment, then asked carefully, "But if I had been testing you . . . ?"

He caught a handful of soft red-gold hair in one fist, pulling her closer to him. "I'm still here."

Inches away from him, she stared into his steady gaze. "So you are."

He kissed her roughly, then pulled away. "Let's go in. I need that drink."

Her irrepressible smile back in full force, she reached for her door handle. "You need tender loving care," she crooned. "Come inside and I'll personally tend to your wounds."

His brow quirked in interest. "Kiss and make better?"

"With pleasure."

He was already feeling a great deal better when he climbed from the car.

HALF AN HOUR LATER they lay on her deep couch, mouths clinging, hands seeking, legs tangled. Growling his need for her, Griff attempted to roll her beneath him, eager to bring their lovemaking to its natural conclusion, all former discomfort wiped out of his mind by her skillful ministrations. She stopped him with one hand, sliding off the couch to stand unselfconsciously nude beside it. "Where are you going?" he demanded gruffly, shoving himself to one elbow as she glided away.

Tossing her tangled hair over one bare shoulder, she smiled at him, kneeling before the stereo. "I'll be right back," she promised.

Impatiently, his damp chest expanding and contracting with ragged breaths, he watched as she selected an album and fitted it carefully onto the turntable. Biting her lip in concentration, she set the tone arm precisely where she wanted it. And then she turned and walked gracefully to him as the voice of Boz Scaggs filled the room, singing the same song they'd heard at the skating rink.

"This is what I wanted to be doing with you while we were skating to this song." Smiling seductively, she joined him on the couch, settling contentedly into his arms.

He cupped her face in one hand, thinking that she'd never looked more beautiful. "I'm almost afraid to admit that we're starting to think alike," he murmured.

Her delighted giggle was lost somewhere in the depths of his mouth as he pulled her beneath him and led them both into the dance of love.

THEY SPENT THE NEXT DAY at Griff's. They both had piles of paperwork to do before Monday morning, so they'd decided to make the task more pleasant by working at the same apartment. Ensconced behind the desk in his study, Griff ploughed through a massive pile of papers. Comfortable in a deep leather wing chair, Melinda concentrated on the portable computer she'd set up on a wooden TV tray Griff had provided. She had no trouble working, but she enjoyed looking up occasionally to admire the way he looked in deep thought, his glasses set squarely on his nose, his dark hair glistening in the overhead light.

At times, he'd look up to find her watching him and his brown eyes would soften, his serious expression changing to a smile. Every time that happened, her heart turned over.

She could get used to being with him like this all the time, she mused.

After several hours, she stored her work and stretched. "I'm thirsty. Want me to bring you a cola?"

"Thanks. That sounds good."

She couldn't help smiling, as she always did, when she walked through Griff's large, luxurious apartment. The decor, as with his office, was elegant, beautifully coordinated, obviously professionally done. Quite a contrast to her own cheerfully eclectic place. Strange how comfortable she was here, despite the differences.

The telephone rang as she poured cola over ice. It rang only once, so she knew Griff had picked it up in the study. Giving him a few minutes for privacy, she rummaged in the pantry and pulled out a bag of chocolate chip cookies. Maybe he'd be in the mood for a snack.

He was still on the phone when she carried in the tray. Hesitating in the doorway, she couldn't help overhearing part of the conversation.

"For the last time, Myers, I'm not defending the guy. No, I don't care that he's one of Dyson's country-club friends. The man's a doctor, and he caused a baby to be born with severe problems just because he didn't consider the poor black mother worthy of his attention when she told him she suspected something was wrong. I've looked over the records, and everything in them indicates to me that he was negligent. He's going to have to find someone else to defend him. Yeah? Well, that's tough. Dyson can choose someone else to take this one. I'm not doing it."

With that, he slammed down the receiver. Only then did he spot Melinda. He ran a hand through his hair, looking uncomfortable. "I do have my standards," he snapped irritably when she didn't say anything.

"I know you do, Griff."

He shifted in the chair. "And don't look at me like I've got some kind of halo hanging over my head, either. I'm still defending Stanley Schulz this week."

"Yes, I know you are."

"You still don't care for what I do," he reminded her, as if it were necessary.

"No, not entirely," she admitted. Swallowing against the tightness in her throat, she smiled. "But I care for you," she dared.

He looked at her for a long time. And then he returned the smile. "My soda's getting warm," he hinted, nodding toward the tray in her hands.

So he wasn't ready to talk about their relationship, she thought, serving him his cola and cookies. But he hadn't seemed disturbed by the implication that her feelings for him were more than casual. There was hope for them yet.

MELINDA COULDN'T RESIST attending one of the court sessions in which Griff defended Stanley Schulz. Though she detested the defendant, though she silently cheered for the families who demanded restitution for their devastating losses, she had to admit that Griff was very, very good at his job. He was fair, she conceded. Though he pulled no punches in his defense, he never deviated from the facts as far as she could ascertain. He simply did his best to persuade the jury to interpret those facts in favor of his client.

A man with honor in a sometimes less than honorable position. A man with standards, regardless that those standards did not always correspond with her own. A man who'd survived a violent, unhappy youth and worked his way up with unfaltering determination, making a life for himself that was working, despite her fears that his repressed bitterness would someday haunt him.

How could she not love him?

Not wanting to distract him, she sat in the very back of the courtroom, slipping out quietly when recess was called. Perhaps she would tell him later that she'd been there, she thought as she started down the hallway toward the exit. And perhaps not.

She hadn't expected to be stopped by a tentative hand on her shoulder. "Excuse me," the dark-haired young man murmured. "My name is Joe McLeod. Would you mind if I ask you a couple of questions?"

Looking at him curiously, she saw a man in his late twenties, sober-faced, in need of a haircut, clad in jeans, a plaid shirt, a casually knotted tie that wasn't a very good match, and a tan sport coat that had seen better days—years earlier. He wasn't wearing any identification, but she pegged him immediately. A reporter. He may as well have been in a uniform.

Her response was cautious. "That depends. What do you want to ask and why?"

"You're the psychologist who testified in the Nancy Hawlsey case, aren't you? I covered that trial and I'm very good with faces."

She'd certainly never expected to be recognized. "Yes, you are good with faces," she acknowledged.

"So you are Melinda James. I thought so." He nodded in satisfaction, then smiled at her narrowed look. "I'm very good with names, too."

"What was it you wanted to ask, Mr. McLeod? I have appointments this afternoon."

"Will you be testifying in this case, Ms. James? Have any of the victims' relatives been under your care?"

"No to both questions. I was here strictly as an observer."

"There must be a reason you're here, Ms. James. How do you feel about this case? Is it your opinion that Stanley Schulz was negligent by not installing a sprinkler system in that building? Do you believe he caused those six deaths with that negligence?"

Edging toward the elevators, she clutched her purse more tightly and wondered if he'd follow if she made a dash for it. "Why in the world would anyone care what my opinions are about this case?"

"I ask for viewpoints from many people, Ms. James. Random samplings of public opinion, you know. It gives me a feel for how the jury may rule. Do you think Stanley Schulz is responsible for the deaths of those six people?"

"Yes, I do," Melinda answered candidly. "I've never considered greed a sufficient defense when people's lives are at stake."

"I find it interesting that you were such a key witness in one case defended by Griffin Taylor and now you're claiming to be nothing more than a curious spectator in a second major trial he's involved in. What do you think about Taylor's almost perfect record of defending wealthy, influential clients in this type of case? Does that record, in your opinion, make him as unethical as you seem to think his clients are?"

Temper flaring, Melinda took another determined step toward the elevator. "Mr. McLeod, I'm not sure what kind of angle you're working, but your questions are hardly those of an unbiased observer. Griffin Taylor is a man who is very good at his job, and his job is to defend his clients. Surely you don't dispute the belief that everyone deserves quality legal defense, regardless of innocence or lack thereof. I respect him for providing that defense to his best abilities. *My* opinions aren't important. It's up to the jury to objectively assess the arguments of both sides of the issue and reach the most equitable conclusion possible. Good bye, Mr. McLeod."

She escaped into the elevator without interference, but she didn't at all like the grin Joe McLeod was wearing as the doors closed between them. She hadn't asked what publication he worked for, she realized in chagrin, morosely picturing the sensationalized scandal sheets that cluttered every supermarket checkout line. Why had McLeod been so fascinated that she'd attended the trial? Why was he asking so many questions about Griff? Had he heard the rumors about Griff's political aspirations and hoped to earn a name for himself with one of those revealing exposés about a political golden boy? Would he—she gulped—would he start to dig into Griff's past?

She should never have attended the trial, she thought regretfully. Her relationship with Griff was still too precarious. What would Wallace Dyson think if he found out that his favorite employee was a former rebel with a questionable reputation, and that he was dating the woman who'd had a part in defeating Dyson and Associates in a case?

Had Dyson noticed that Griff hadn't been out with Leslie lately—and was Griff ready to sever that connection completely? She knew he hadn't seen Leslie since the night of the charity auction, but he'd never told Melinda that he wouldn't see Leslie again. Not that she'd asked, of course. They hadn't quite reached that stage.

She really wished she'd resisted the temptation to watch him at work. Griff would probably be very annoyed that she had.

It wasn't until much later that afternoon that Melinda realized how heatedly she'd defended Griff's profession to the pushy reporter. And she'd used Griff's arguments to do so.

No wonder he swayed so many juries to his side, she thought ruefully, absently rubbing a fingertip over her lower lip. He was one highly persuasive man. A person would have to be very careful with a man like that. Or she might find herself in danger of questioning her own opinions, her right to independent and opposite beliefs.

This was all getting very complicated, she thought with a low moan, rubbing her temples as she waited for the clinic receptionist to bring in her last appointment for the day.

9

"GRIFF, YOU REALLY DON'T have to come with me to-night. After all, you don't even live in River City."

Easily guiding his car through early-evening traffic, Griff chuckled and shot her a quick, sideways glance. "And miss seeing you take on an entire city council meeting? No way."

Melinda fidgeted nervously in the passenger seat. "Um—Griff, you know sometimes when I'm defending something I truly believe in—well, I tend to get a little . . . passionate."

"I like it when you get passionate."

She sighed at his deliberate misinterpretation of her meaning. "What I'm trying to say is, I don't want to embarrass you tonight. But I'm not going to sit back and be quiet while the city council considers an ordinance that is censorship at its most obscene."

"Nor do I expect you to," he returned mildly. "Stop worrying about it, Melinda. You won't embarrass me."

She hoped not. She really did. She still hadn't had the nerve to tell him about her run-in with the nosy reporter earlier that week. Considering herself fortunate that her comments hadn't appeared in print anywhere as far as she could tell, she'd decided to wait until just the right time to break it to Griff that there was a hungry young reporter out there with an eye on a juicy story. Armed with a pen with Griff's name on it.

Griff seemed to enjoy the next two hours, to Melinda's amazement. As she'd warned him, she was a highly vocal participant in the heated debate that began the moment the proposed ordinance was opened for debate. Sponsored by a local fundamentalist group, the ordinance was a blatant attempt to ban the sale or rental of all books, magazines, videotapes and audiotapes the group found offensive. Concerned about their political futures if it was perceived that they were promoting the distribution of so-called adult material, the council members found themselves caught between their belief in the First Amendment and the urgings of their pastors and grandmothers.

"And just who will decide what material is offensive?" Melinda challenged at one point, her supporters cheering her on as the council squirmed miserably at the front of the crowded room. "Some people are offended by R-rated movies, others by PG-13 films."

"Any film that isn't suitable for an entire family shouldn't be made in the first place," one of the more rabid, offensively sanctimonious proponents of the ordinance interrupted.

"I'm not going to argue the merits of individual films with you," Melinda replied coolly, ignoring the glare of camera flashes from the reporters and photographers covering the controversial meeting. "I'm simply saying that not everyone agrees on what is or is not offensive or pornographic. Look at the movements to ban certain books from school libraries and classrooms— books that are considered by many to be great works of literature. We can all agree that there are publications that border the edges of illegality, but some people would say the same about many of the controversial, sexually explicit books that are considered perfectly respectable best-sellers."

The man who'd interrupted Melinda earlier, a flamboyant, publicity loving leader of a local morality movement, ran a hand through his dramatically styled silver hair and turned to the council members. With an exaggerated swing of one arm, he tossed a stack of magazines on the table in front of the mayor. "Look at this filth," he declared in ringing, stage-quality outrage. "I myself purchased these magazines at various establishments throughout our city. I have never been so disgusted in my life. Is this what we want our children to be exposed to in their precious formative years?"

"Hey, pass those around, will you, Mayor?" a young male voice yelled from the back of the room, causing an outbreak of laughter.

Griff chuckled quietly from his seat at Melinda's side, where he'd sat in silent observation since the meeting began.

"Yeah—after he looks at all of 'em," another man retorted.

Red-faced, the mayor, whom Melinda had always considered an unqualified, ineffective leader, pounded the table. "Let's have some order in here," he demanded, though his tone was more that of a plea.

Melinda was ready with a response. "Whatever my own opinion of those publications, the Supreme Court has ruled that they are protected by the First Amendment. And children aren't allowed to buy them, anyway."

"The Supreme Court is run by a bunch of pinko liberals—like you," someone shouted belligerently.

Melinda whirled for a confrontation, but Griff caught her arm. "Don't waste your breath arguing with the crazies," he advised quietly, his face very close to hers. A flashbulb caught the smile he gave her, but he ignored it. "You're doing fine. Don't let them rattle you."

Nodding, she took a deep breath and summed up the arguments of the opponents to the ordinance, a citizen's group that had elected her their spokesperson prior to the meeting. It was all she could do to sit quietly while the silver-haired spokesman for the other side made his case. It helped that Griff reached out and took her hand, holding it warmly throughout the rest of the hearing.

By the time the meeting came to an end, the ordinance had been watered down to nothing more than a reinforcement of laws already in existence that forbade the sale or rental of adult materials to minors. Melinda had no argument with that, though she considered the entire evening a waste of the taxpayers' money. The ordinance should never have been considered, she told Griff in a disgruntled mutter as he headed the car in the direction of her apartment.

Agreeing, he gave her a smile that warmed her all the way through. "I was impressed with your arguments, Melinda. You stayed calm, rational and logical. You probably missed your calling, you know. You'd have made a hell of an attorney."

She flinched. He chuckled at her look of horror. "It's not as if I'd suggested you'd make a good prostitute," he told her in mild amusement.

Concerned that she might have offended him with her unguarded reaction, she hurriedly apologized. "It's just that I love what I do now," she explained. "I can't imagine being anything else."

He nodded. "I'm sure you're very good at what you do. You're a good listener. People probably have no problem pouring out all their troubles to you."

She tilted her head in question, wondering if there'd been just a trace of condescension in his voice. Almost as if what she did was an interesting hobby, but not exactly something to be taken seriously. And then she decided that she was being overly defensive. Griff had never said anything specifically to make her believe he felt that way. In fact, he'd been surprisingly tolerant of her little eccentricities. Had never made any effort to change her into a more conforming, more suitable mate for a political aspirant.

Which only made her wonder if he hadn't tried to change her because he didn't foresee having her in his future.

Oh, great, Melinda. Now you're getting paranoid, she told herself impatiently.

But then again, maybe there really was something to worry about.

LYING ON HIS SIDE, propped on one elbow, Griff rested his head in his hand and watched Melinda sleep. Sometimes he was content to do nothing more than simply look at her. She was so very beautiful. It wasn't her features, exactly, he decided, trying to analyze why her face was more fascinating to him than the face of any other woman he'd known. It had more to do with an almost palpable glow about her, as if her personality was so vital, so dynamic, so very much alive that it radiated from her even in repose. He'd never known anyone who faced life with more intensity, more reckless fervor. After so many years of being careful, he found her enthusiasm contagious.

She was turning his life upside down. And he found himself capable of doing nothing but holding on and enjoying the ride.

He couldn't imagine going back to his life before she'd come into it. His routine had been safer, perhaps, more predictable. Yet so much less interesting. When was the last time he'd had fun before Melinda? He couldn't even remember. With her, fun was a part of his life again. It was as if he'd had to learn how to play at thirty.

And yet it wasn't all games, he realized. They'd had some very lengthy, serious, thought-provoking conversations. She hadn't been playing at that city council meeting earlier. She'd been deadly serious in her opposition to an ordinance that she saw as dangerous and suppressive. Melinda would always be one who'd throw herself wholeheartedly into any conflict in which she took a passionate stand.

He could live with that.

That last thought made him frown. *Could* he live with that? he asked himself, trying to be more cautious in his deepening involvement with her. Was he willing to take the risks? His life was already changing because of her. Dyson had made a few veiled remarks about

Griff's recent unavailability for several social functions, a few not-so-subtle hints that Griff should call Leslie again.

Griff had made no effort to attend those social functions with Melinda at his side. He still wasn't sure why. Was it because he hadn't thought she'd enjoy them? Or—he thought with great reluctance—had he been concerned that she'd say something, do something that would be detrimental to his position with the firm? Surely he wasn't that much of a coward. Was he? And surely his position wouldn't be affected by his choice of companions. Would it? He'd worked very hard to attain his position. He'd earned it. His involvement with Melinda shouldn't change anything concerning his job. He'd known all along that involvement with Melinda James would not be without risks. And yet he hadn't seemed able—or willing—to avoid that involvement. Was this love he felt for her? This need to be with her, this pleasure he felt in lying beside her, watching her sleep?

And if it was, just how much was he willing to sacrifice in the name of love?

MELINDA HAD JUST GOTTEN HOME from her office the next day when the doorbell rang. Since she was expecting Griff to pick her up for dinner, she opened the door eagerly.

"Don't you ever ask who's on the other side before you pull that door open?" the dark-haired man standing on her doorstep demanded.

"Now where have I heard that question before?" Melinda mused aloud then broke into a broad grin.

"What on earth are you doing here? Did Brooke throw you out?"

Her brother reciprocated with his attractive smile. "You know better than that. My wife's crazy about me."

"Yes, I know. I've just never quite understood why." She reached out to give him an enthusiastic hug. "It's good to see you."

Matt returned the hug warmly, their habitual bantering set aside for a moment to express the genuine affection that lay beneath it. "It's good to see you, too. I'd see a bit less of you, however, if you'd fasten two more buttons on that blouse," he added with a mock scowl as he set her away from him.

Rolling her eyes, she pulled him inside, her red silk blouse remaining exactly the way she'd had it. "Are you always going to treat me like a kid?"

"Probably. It's my prerogative as an older brother."

Settling beside him on her couch, she took a moment to study him. At thirty-seven, Matt was still trim and terribly handsome, his glossy near-black hair silvered only a bit at the temples. He had the same emerald-green, unusually uptilted eyes as Melinda, their mother's eyes, which all but one of the five siblings had inherited. "You look good, Matt. Still working out, I see."

"I have to, just to keep up with Rachel. The kid never runs out of energy. She and Brooke both send their love, by the way."

Unable to restrain herself any longer, Melinda asked, "What *are* you doing here? You're supposed to be at your resort in Nashville."

"I arrived in St. Louis this morning. Spent the afternoon with that architect you mentioned last time we talked."

"So you did call him. Was he as wonderful as I said?"

"He had some really good ideas for designing the cocktail lounge Ken and I want to add to the resort," Matt admitted. "I was impressed."

"Why didn't you tell me you were going to be here? And why didn't you bring Brooke and Rachel?"

"Rachel's best friend had a birthday party tonight that Rachel just couldn't bear to miss. I'm flying back first thing in the morning. Thought I'd surprise you and take you out on the town tonight. What do you say?"

She sighed in resignation at his typically arrogant gesture. "And if I already have plans?"

"Break them," he returned without hesitation, his smile smug. "Tell the poor, besotted lad you can't see him tonight because your long-lost brother is in town."

"I have a better idea. Let's ask him to join us."

Matt made a face. "Spare me. I don't think I can take another entire evening watching you break some poor lovesick guy's heart while you tantalize him with your restless-butterfly routine."

Startled by his description of her behavior, Melinda shook her head forcefully. "How can you say that? I don't do that."

"Of course you do. According to Merry, you haven't let any guy tie you down to more than a few dates in years. I realize that you place great value on your independence, Melinda, but you'd better start thinking about settling down. You're not getting any younger, you know."

Managing a weak smile at his teasing, Melinda decided to have a long talk with her older sister about discussing her with their brother. "This one's different, Matt. He's . . . special."

Reading something in her tone, Matt studied her intently. "Yeah? How special?"

"Very special."

He winced. "He's not one of those oddball psychologists you hang out with, is he?"

"He's not a psychologist."

"Some other type of oddball, then." He made a show of steeling himself for bad news. "What does he do?"

Melinda wondered what Matt would say if she confided that she was seeing Savage, whom Matt had vehemently and repeatedly forbidden her to date. In vain. Though tempted, she decided not to tell him just yet. "He's an attorney."

"One of those wild, storefront types, right? Cheap plaid suits and more *pro bono* clients than paying ones? Or one of those liberal, intense union guys?"

Smiling to herself, Melinda shook her head. "Corporate. Very conservative."

Matt snorted. "Yeah, sure. Something tells me that your idea of conservative varies quite a bit from mine."

The doorbell chimed and Melinda stood. "You can judge for yourself," she informed him cheerfully. "That will be Griff."

Matt moaned. "Griff?" he muttered. "What kind of a name is Griff?"

You could always call him Savage, she almost said, but refrained. Pulling open the door, she smiled at the man standing there. "Hi."

"Someday we are going to have to have a long talk about this habit you have of just opening the door any time the bell rings," Griff announced firmly. And then he pulled her to him for a lingering kiss. "Hi," he said when he released her.

"Well, at least he sounds like a man with common sense," Matt observed from the couch.

At the unfamiliar male voice coming from Melinda's living room, Griff lifted his head with a quick frown, giving her a narrowed look of question. She rather enjoyed the unmistakable possessiveness in that look, though she wasn't too sure about the almost military stance he'd adopted. As if he were ready to eliminate the invader and then issue her a concise list of rules for future reference.

Deciding to defuse the situation with a bright smile and cheery tone, she took Griff's hand and turned with him to Matt. "Griff, I'd like you to meet my brother, Matt James. Matt, this is Griff Taylor, the attorney I was just telling you about."

Griff shot Melinda a rather startled look at her wording of the introduction to a man he'd once known, however briefly. And then he seemed to grasp her game. To her startled pleasure, a look of near mischief glinted in his brown eyes before they turned to her brother. Extending his hand, he nodded amiably to the older man. "Nice to meet you, Matt."

Matt studied Melinda's date as he returned the handshake. Melinda tried to keep from laughing aloud at the wary approval in her brother's expression. It was obvious that he hadn't been expecting a clean-cut, classically handsome man in glasses and a conventional, tailored dark suit. "Melinda tells me you're a corporate attorney."

"Yes, Dyson and Associates is retained by a number of prominent corporations," Griff affirmed.

Matt's brow rose higher. "Dyson and Associates? I've heard of the firm."

"I understand you own a resort in Nashville. Melinda's told me that it's a very nice place to vacation."

"My partner and I would be glad to have you visit us there sometime."

Griff smiled at Melinda. "Maybe I will."

"Matt's planning to build a cocktail lounge at the resort," Melinda explained. "He was in St. Louis today to talk to Alan Burnett about designing it for him."

"Burnett's a brilliant architect," Griff responded with a nod. "He and I belong to the same country club."

"Country club, huh?" Matt repeated in a murmur, sending his sister a quizzical glance.

Ignoring the look, she continued her explanation of Matt's presence. "Matt decided to surprise me and take me out to dinner. He didn't think it necessary to check with me first about my plans," she was unable to resist adding.

"No problem," Griff said equably. Turning to Matt, he smiled. "We'd be delighted to have you join us this evening. We thought we'd try a new Chinese restaurant that's supposed to be very good."

"Thanks, I love Chinese food." Matt hesitated a moment. "You know, you look vaguely familiar. Have we met before?"

Griff's smile never wavered. "I suppose it's possible."

Still looking thoughtful, Matt shook his head. "I can't place you just now. Maybe it'll come to me later."

Griff murmured something noncommittal. To hide her expression, Melinda turned to find her purse. Brushing a nonexistent speck of lint from her narrow, pleated black slacks, she waited until her amusement was under control before turning with a jingle of gold chains and heavy gold earrings. "Two good-looking men at my side," she said, taking Griff's arm and reaching for Matt's. "I've always enjoyed that type of evening."

Matt looked suspicious of the compliment. As for Griff, he did not look particularly amused by her suggestion.

Melinda laughed and prepared herself for a very entertaining evening.

By the time they'd finished their appetizers and started on the main course, Matt was thoroughly won over by Melinda's date. "Have you two been seeing each other long?" he asked, beginning what Melinda knew would become a brotherly inquisition.

"Quite a while," Griff replied vaguely, deftly catching a sauce-coated shrimp between his chopsticks.

"You've spent a lot of time with my sister?"

Griff's mouth twitched. "Yes, as much as possible in spite of our heavy work schedules."

Matt feigned bewilderment. "And you still want to date her?"

"Matt," Melinda protested.

"You are aware," Matt continued to Griff, "that Melinda doesn't really think like other people? To put it bluntly, she's a flake."

"Matt!"

Griff chased down a snow pea and replied easily. "Yes, I'm aware of that."

Melinda set her chopsticks down abruptly. "Griff!"

"I could tell you stories that would chill your blood," Matt went on, obviously enjoying himself greatly.

Griff looked interested. "For example?"

"Well, there was the time she—"

"Both of you can just stop this right now," Melinda interrupted firmly. "It's unfair. I'm outnumbered."

Her brother shrugged. "I can't help it. Griff seems like a nice guy. He deserves to be warned about what he's getting into."

"I appreciate that," Griff answered gravely. "But I'm fully aware of the risks."

"And you seem so normal." Matt shook his head again as if to indicate that the situation was beyond his comprehension.

Melinda had had enough. "Oh, yeah? What about the red satin and black lace bikini underwear he has on under that suit?"

Griff choked violently on a mouthful of vegetables and reached hastily for his water glass. "Dammit, Melinda!" he scolded the moment his mouth was free, his cheeks rather pink.

"Why is it that both you and Matt seem compelled to preface my name with that particular expletive?" she asked, rhetorically, satisfied with her minor revenge.

"You're lucky neither of us has turned you over our knee," Matt commented, struggling with a smile at Griff's embarrassment.

"Both of you have threatened, but neither has had the nerve to try."

"You, too, huh?"

Griff nodded in response to Matt's sympathetic question.

"I can't believe the two of you are getting along like this," Melinda complained, picking up her chopsticks again to attack her dinner. "Who'd have ever dreamed you'd end up so much alike?"

Matt looked puzzled. "What?"

"She has this tendency to babble when she's annoyed," Griff interjected quickly before Melinda could speak.

She glared at him, but Matt seemed satisfied by the explanation. "Yes, she does, doesn't she? You know, this food is really good. How's yours, Griff?"

Griff fell right in with Matt's change of subject. "Not bad. A bit too heavy on the ginger, but other than that it's fine."

"If you're ever in Nashville, I'll have to take you to my favorite Chinese restaurant. I can guarantee the kung pao chicken is the best you've ever tasted."

"I may take you up on that."

Matt paused with a bit of pork halfway to his mouth. Lowering it, he cleared his throat. "There's just one thing I need to know before we go any further with this friendship."

"White cotton briefs," Griff muttered into an egg roll.

Matt grinned. "I can't tell you what a relief that is." He popped the meat into his mouth and chewed with apparent pleasure.

Looking from her brother to her lover, Melinda sighed deeply and concentrated on her meal. She was pleased that Matt and Griff seemed to be getting along so well, of course. But did they have to be quite so enthusiastic about it?

THEY WERE HAVING COFFEE and conversation at Melinda's apartment when Matt shook his head, looking at Griff with a slight frown. "You know, I still have this feeling we've met before. I'm usually pretty good with faces, but I can't decide why you look so familiar. Where are you from originally?"

Melinda sat back with a smile and motioned for Griff to answer as he saw fit.

Griff grimaced at her, then took a deep breath. She knew he was reluctant to explain. He'd seemed to enjoy his fresh start with Matt, unspoiled by the memories he was so determined to avoid. "I'm from Springfield."

"Springfield, Missouri?" Matt clarified, startled by the name of his hometown.

"That's right."

Matt cocked his head, setting his coffee cup on the table beside his chair. "So we *have* met before. But I . . . The only Taylor I remember . . ." He paused, his eyes widening. "Oh, no. You couldn't be." He looked at Melinda.

She nodded contentedly. "Yes, he could. Still going to tell me I can't go out with him, Matt? I warn you, I'm not going to obey you this time, either."

Matt shoved a hand through his hair and turned his accusing gaze to Griff. "You're the kid who used to call himself Savage?"

"Well, I'm not a kid any more."

"The guy with the long hair and the earrings and—"

"And the bad reputation," Griff finished flatly.

"I didn't recognize him, either," Melinda put in. "Like you, I thought he looked familiar at first, but then he attacked me and I got so mad I forgot about it."

"He *attacked* you?"

"She was a witness for the other side against one of my clients in court."

Matt drummed his fingers against the arm of his chair, giving Griff another long inspection. "So you're Savage," he murmured at length.

"No," Griff denied, voice clipped. "That's all in the past. Everything's changed now. *I've* changed."

"I can see that."

"Believe it. There's nothing left of the kid you remember. I left him behind when I left Springfield."

Matt's frown deepened at Griff's terse vehemence. "Maybe I overreacted when you and Melinda were dating before," he confessed. "I was still pretty young and I took my responsibilities to my younger sisters very seriously. Merry always thought you were a nice guy. She wouldn't be surprised that you turned out this way."

"You didn't overreact. I wouldn't let a daughter or sister of mine date a guy like that, either,'" Griff replied with an attempt at a smile. "I'm just glad I managed to turn myself around before it was too late."

Listening silently, Melinda worried her bottom lip with her teeth, concerned at Griff's continued refusal to accept his past. This was it, she realized, her hands clenching in her lap. This was what had been bothering her so much about their relationship. The issue of his past—of *their* past—was still hanging over them like the sword of Damocles, poised to sever the tentative bonds that had developed over the past weeks. Until they had come to terms with that past, together, it still held the potential to hurt them.

Seeming to sense Griff's reluctance to reminisce, Matt obligingly changed the subject. Though Melinda found it hard to participate with her full attention, she joined in the polite conversation for the next hour. And then Matt glanced at his watch. "I'd better go. It's getting late."

"You're staying here, aren't you?" Melinda asked, surprised that he'd consider any other option.

He shook his head. "I've got a room in a hotel near the airport in St. Louis. I'm booked on an early flight and that will be more convenient for both of us."

Griff immediately stood and reached for the jacket he'd discarded when they'd returned to the apartment. "I'll drive you."

"Not necessary. I have a rental car. It was more convenient than catching cabs all day. But thanks. I appreciate the offer."

Griff held out his hand, his smile genuine. "I enjoyed the evening, Matt. We'll have to get together sometime."

The handshake was firm. "It may be a while before I get back to this area." Though the statement was hardly a question, both Melinda and Griff immediately understood what Matt was asking.

Griff's smile deepened as his eyes lingered on Melinda for a meaningful moment. "I'll still be around."

Melinda's knees weakened. It took only that to make her almost forget all her doubts about their relationship, she thought gravely.

Matt seemed satisfied—and pleased. He turned to Melinda, jerking his chin toward Griff. "I never thought I'd say this to you, kid, but I approve of the guy. Try to hold on to this one, will you?"

Deciding to leave that alone, she linked her arms around his neck and kissed his cheek. "Have a safe trip. I loved seeing you, but give me a call next time, will you? I'd hate to have missed you."

"We'll see each other again in—what is it, three weeks until Thanksgiving?"

"Something like that."

"Merry can't wait to have everyone together for another weekend. And there's always room for one more," he hinted, the comment intended for both Melinda and Griff.

Melinda and Griff only smiled noncommittally. They hadn't talked about Thanksgiving plans yet, though Melinda had fully intended to invite Griff to join her in Springfield. She'd wondered if he would accept, or if he would still refuse to return to the town where he'd grown up.

"I don't think I'll tell the others who you're dating," Matt said as he left. "I want to be around when they find out for themselves." He was smiling in anticipation when Melinda shut the door behind him.

Two arms immediately circled her waist from behind. "I enjoyed the evening, but I've been going crazy for the past hour wanting to hold you," Griff murmured, lowering his head to nibble at her ear. "Did I remember to tell that you look exceptionally beautiful tonight?"

"You tell me that every time you see me," she replied huskily, her hands covering his at her waist as she leaned against him.

"That's because it's always true. You're beautiful."

Turning in his arms, she linked her hands behind his head. "Flatterer."

"No. Just an objective observer."

She scoffed at his use of the word "objective," though he gravely assured her that he wasn't at all biased by the fact that they were lovers. And then he kissed her and the mock disagreement ended.

Melinda was able to pull away before the kisses burned out of control—just barely. "Griff, we have to talk." Her voice was a bit ragged around the edges, but she was determined.

He stiffened immediately, and she knew he wasn't going to like what she had to say. "About what?"

"About the past. About Savage."

He exhaled forcefully, half turning away from her to rub irritably at the back of his neck. "Oh, hell."

She crossed her arms at her waist, bereft at the loss of the intimate mood they'd shared only moments before. And terribly afraid that forcing a confrontation would damage the intimacy permanently. But she had no choice. She couldn't go on any longer waiting for the worst to happen.

She was fighting, this time, for the most important objective she'd ever targeted. A future with Griff.

10

GRIFF TURNED TO MELINDA with stiff shoulders, braced for a quarrel. "I suppose you're going to insist on getting into this now?"

"I'm afraid so." She attempted a smile. "I just want to talk to you, Griff. Is that so terrible?"

"It is if you're still determined to rake up the past. I can't understand why you're so obsessed with the subject. It's not as if it has anything to do with our relationship now."

"How can you say that? It has a great deal to do with us. We shared that past, at least a small part of it. If we can't enjoy reminiscing over those memories, then we're pretending we just met a few months ago. You can't base a relationship on a pretense."

He scowled and dropped into the chair Matt had vacated, legs thrust out in front of him. "I've never pretended anything with you. I just see no need to dwell on unpleasant memories."

"You keep saying that," she said quietly, her arms tightening around her waist. "Am I a part of your unpleasant memories? I thought we had some wonderful times together."

He pulled off his glasses and rubbed the back of his hand over his face, the gesture weary and dispirited. "Maybe there were some good times," he admitted.

"But I can't think of them without remembering the bad times, as well. And it's just too hard to think about those bad times. It hurts too much." The last words were barely audible. He didn't look at her as he said them.

Her heart twisting, Melinda knelt beside his chair, resting her hand on his notably taut arm. "Oh, Griff, I know it hurts. Don't you know how badly I hate that for you?"

"Then, dammit, why do you keep bringing it up?" he exploded, his fist clenching. "Why can't you just let me leave it buried?"

"Because the memories aren't going to stay buried. You can't deny the events in your past that made you what you are. You can't pretend they never happened, because someday you're going to have to face them. Maybe someone will find out about them and start asking questions. Or maybe you'll be haunted by dreams— I've seen that happen so many times with repression."

His arm jerked beneath her hand. Had he been having dreams? she wondered, aching for him. Was he already being tormented by the demons that would never leave him alone until he'd conquered them? "What do you want me to do?" Griff asked in a near growl, eyeing her warily.

She took a deep breath. "It's not so bad, really. We can talk about the past, about your feelings then and now. Your feelings about your mother, about your father."

"My mother ran out on me when I was ten. I don't even know if she's still alive. She left me with a drunken son of a bitch who got his kicks out of knocking me around until I got big enough to threaten to beat him senseless. How do you think I feel about them?" His voice was bitter, sarcastic.

"Why don't you tell me?"

He pulled his arm from beneath her hand and shoved himself out of the chair. "Oh, great. Just what I need. Some of your psycho-babble therapy. I'm not one of your fruitcake patients, Melinda. Let me take care of my own problems, would you?"

Even though she knew he was lashing out at her in response to his own pain and confusion, his words still stung, particularly since she'd wondered before exactly how he felt about her profession. It seemed he didn't have a great deal of respect for it. She tried to keep the hurt out of her voice as she stood and faced him squarely. "I'm only trying to help, Griff."

"I suppose I would be grateful if I *needed* help," he answered shortly. "I don't."

"So you want me to just stand by and watch as you continue to live this—this masquerade? To continue to repress any part of yourself that reminds you too much of Savage? To force yourself into a mold just to please and impress other people?"

He kept his expression unreadable during her questioning. When she finished, he spoke very quietly. "I've told you before, Melinda, that if we're going to make this thing work between us, you're going to have to accept me the way I am."

"How can I accept you when you've never learned to accept yourself?" she asked sadly. "You act as though you're ashamed of your past, of the person you were, even of the things—like your parents' actions—over which you had no control."

"I'm hardly proud of my past."

"You should be proud of who you are—what you've made of yourself because of that past. I happen to think Savage was a wonderful person, an honest, uncompromising, unpretentious young man who made me feel so honored to be his friend."

A muscle in his jaw twitched. He shoved his hands in his packets. "You sound as though you still prefer that guy to me."

"Dammit, Griff!" Too frustrated to recognize the irony of the familiar wording, she barely resisted the impulse to clench her fists in her hair in exasperation. "That guy *is* you. You can't keep denying that you are Savage, that he'll always be a part of you."

He drew a deep breath and shook his head. "We keep coming back to that, don't we? We talk and talk and always end up saying the same things."

"That's because we've never resolved them. The problems are still there, regardless of how long or how hard we try to ignore them."

"So where does that leave us?"

"I don't know," she admitted candidly. "I want to work this out. I want to keep seeing you without fear that I might say something to annoy you by reminding you of the past. To be able to share my feelings with you and have you do the same with me. I want to be able to ask you to spend Thanksgiving with me and my family without worrying about how you'll react to the idea of going back to Springfield and spending time with people who remember you as Savage."

Attention arrested, he frowned. "You want me to go home with you for Thanksgiving?"

"Of course I do. I want more than anything to spend that holiday with you and my family."

He raised his right hand to knead the back of his neck again in that gesture she recognized as a sign of stress. "I hadn't planned to ever go back there."

"I know you hadn't. You hadn't planned on having me come back into your life, either."

"No."

She didn't want to ask the question. She really didn't. And yet she heard it coming out, anyway. "Are you sorry I did?"

Being Griff, he took his time to carefully consider the question before answering. Though she might have wished he could have replied without any hesitation, she knew that she could trust the answer he would give to be the truth, and not just whatever he thought she wanted to hear. With her, at least, he'd always been honest—painfully honest, at times.

He'd just opened his mouth to speak when the telephone rang. Her first impulse was to ignore it and continue her confrontation with Griff uninterrupted. But it was late—too late for social calls.

"You'd better get that," Griff urged, nodding toward the ringing phone. "It may be important."

She hesitated only a moment longer, then picked up the receiver.

Hands in his pockets, Griff watched as she half turned away, her attention obviously divided between him and the telephone. And then her expression changed and he knew the call was serious. His first thought was of her family. Had something happened to one of them? Had Matt been involved in an accident on his way to his hotel?

The extent of his concern, of his growing involvement with Melinda and her family, left him feeling confused, disconcerted. He was beginning to realize that if he went any further in his relationship with Melinda, he was going to have to face his past, whether he wanted to or not. Involvement with Melinda necessarily included her family. A future with her would mean numerous visits in Springfield, breaking the solemn vow he'd made years ago to never set foot in that city again.

Maybe it was time to reassess that vow.

"I'll be right there," he heard Melinda say before she replaced the receiver. And then she turned to him, her eyes troubled, her expression grave. "I have to leave."

"What is it?"

Chewing her lower lip in the gesture he recognized as a sign of anxiety, she looked around for her purse. "One of my patients has been hurt," she explained, finding her purse and digging in it for her keys. "Very badly hurt. She's asking for me. I have to go to her."

"Where is she?"

"Memorial Hospital."

He reached for his jacket. "I'll take you."

"That's not necessary. I can—"

He took her keys out of her hand. "I said I'll take you. It's too late for you to be out running around by yourself."

Her response to Griff's high-handed remark was a mere grimace.

She was very quiet during the ride to the hospital. After a glance at her pale, set face, Griff asked, "Is this patient very special to you?"

She pushed her hair away from her face. "All my patients are special to me. But this one..." Her voice trailed away.

"A young person?"

"She's a couple of years younger than I am. Very sweet, very trusting. Too trusting."

"What happened to her?"

"She was beaten." Her voice was edged with pain. "I don't know who did it. She works in a dive in a really bad part of town, so it could have been a mugging—or rape. And she has a boyfriend who's hit her a few times, though never badly enough to require medical attention."

Griff remembered all too well what it was like to be at the receiving end of an anger-driven fist. Feeling vulnerable and impotent. "Sounds like she leads a rough life," was all he said.

"Yes. Yes, she does. But it's the only life she knows. She's afraid to walk away from it, no matter how many times I've urged her to get help."

"Yeah, well, it's easier to tell someone what she should do than it is to be in the situation yourself."

"I'm aware of that," Melinda answered almost inaudibly.

He winced as he realized what he'd said. "I wasn't criticizing you."

She didn't answer. She still hadn't spoken when they entered the hospital emergency room.

Griff stayed right at her heels as she inquired about her patient and then hurried to the room to which she was directed. No one tried to stop him. Perhaps the expression he wore made it clear they'd be wasting their time. Melinda might need him. He intended to be there for her if she did.

Melinda froze in the doorway with an audible catch of her breath when she saw the young woman lying on the narrow bed. His hands squeezing her shoulders, Griff understood her distress. The woman was a mess, her limp, bleached hair matted with blood, tangled around a face that might have been attractive had it not been so swollen and discolored with bruises and cuts. An IV needle had been taped to one arm; the other arm lay at her side, splinted as though for a fracture. Taking a deep breath, Melinda looked over her shoulder at Griff. "Please stay back."

"I won't get in your way," he assured her, stepping back for emphasis.

She nodded and turned to the bed, approaching slowly. The nurse who'd been standing beside the bed stepped away. Melinda spoke quietly. "Twyla?"

The woman opened her eyes as much as their obviously painful swelling would permit. "Ms. James?" Her voice was little more than a raw whisper.

"Yes, Twyla, it's Melinda. I'm so sorry you've been hurt."

"Thanks for coming. I know it's late and I shouldn't have asked them to call you, but I don't have anyone else and I—"

"No, Twyla. I'm glad you had them call me," Melinda interrupted firmly. "I'd like to think we've become friends and friends should be together at a time like this."

Twyla's breath caught in a harsh sob. "Oh, Ms. James. It was Jim. He just went crazy. He—oh, God, he hurt me so bad."

Eyes glistening with tears, Melinda leaned down to rest her cheek against the woman's dirty, blood-caked hair. "You don't have to talk about it now, Twyla. Just get some rest and let these people take care of you."

Knowing his presence was superfluous, Griff slipped out the door, leaving Melinda to do what she did best. Be a friend.

A very special woman, his Melinda, he mused as he sipped an incredibly bad cup of coffee in the hospital canteen. A heart as big as the sky, open to people in trouble, people in pain. She'd been that way at four-teen, sensing Griff's loneliness and pain, offering friendship and unconditional acceptance. She hadn't changed nearly as much as he had.

He should have remembered to thank her for that friendship during the past few weeks, rather than let her go on thinking that he had nothing but ugly memories of that earlier time. He should have told her that he owed much of what he'd made of himself to her. She'd championed him when no one else had, made him be-lieve that he could be someone, that he deserved better than what he'd been given. Because of her faith in him, he'd made a vow to prove her right. And he had.

Yet, instead of thanking her, he'd rejected her at first and then, when he'd been unable to stay away from her, he'd taken her with the implicit understanding that the past was taboo, a subject neither of them would mention. He'd shared her bed, but withheld his deepest feelings from her. Knowing Melinda, he realized how much that must have hurt her. And yet she hadn't given up on him. She'd kept at him to share himself with her, though she'd known she risked his anger, perhaps even risked their relationship. Because she worried about him. Because she cared for him. Maybe she even loved him.

Love. He was in love with Melinda James. So deeply in love that he hadn't thought clearly since the first time he'd kissed her. He'd convinced himself that they could go on just as they had been, pretending they'd only just met, pretending there were no dark shadows lurking behind their lighthearted play. He'd kept her from his professional life, hiding her away as if ashamed to be seen with her, when the truth was that his proudest moments were those spent at her side. Yet he'd never told her.

He'd started out trying to make her like him again. Now he wondered at his arrogance in demanding that she like a man who didn't like himself very much. And the more he looked at himself, the less he found to like.

It wasn't his job. It bothered him that Melinda didn't approve of what he did, but he honestly believed that his profession was an honorable one when practiced with honor. And he'd always taken pride in doing just that. His clients may not always have been right, they may not always have been completely ethical in their business dealings, but they deserved a fair trial and quality representation. The juries were responsible for deciding punishment or exoneration. Perhaps in the future he'd be somewhat less reticent with his own opinions, but he had no intention of giving up his career. That would be something Melinda would have to learn to accept, just as he'd have to understand that she would always be available to her patients when they needed her, as she had been tonight.

No, it wasn't his job. But the things he'd done to succeed in that job—the evasions, the pretenses, the times he'd swallowed his opinions to imply that he agreed with the majority—he was hardly proud of those. Hell, he'd even toyed with the idea of marrying a woman he didn't love to insure his own successful future. Had Melinda not come along when she did, he may well have made that reprehensible decision. And in his infinite arrogance, *he'd* criticized *her* for being herself— uninhibited, spontaneous, opinionated, deeply committed to the people and causes she believed in. The very things he'd grown to love about her.

"What a jerk," he muttered, staring glumly into the murky dregs of his coffee.

"Who's a jerk?" The softly spoken question brought his head up sharply. Melinda was standing beside his table, her smile rather weak, eyes a bit red-rimmed, so tired she was almost swaying on her feet. Glancing at his watch, he realized he'd been sitting at that table for over an hour, lost in his own self-censure.

"How's Twyla?" he asked, pushing away from the table.

"Sleeping. She'll be okay after a few days of recuperation. I told her I'd come to see her tomorrow."

He nodded and draped an arm around her shoulders. "Let's get you home to bed. You're exhausted."

She nestled against him in an instinctively trusting gesture that made his throat tighten. "I am tired," she murmured with a sigh. "Poor Twyla. What I'd like to do to that bastard who did this to her!" She looked at Griff as they walked toward the exit. "Too bad you're not a prosecuting attorney. I'd urge you to push for the electric chair for the creep."

"You don't even believe in capital punishment," he reminded her, wrapping her coat more tightly around her as they stepped into the cool night air.

"I know. I'm just mad."

"I don't blame you. By the way, did they arrest the guy?"

"Yeah. Twyla said she's definitely pressing charges this time. I think she will."

"Good." He helped her into his car, then walked around to slide behind the wheel.

Melinda leaned back against the seat, eyes closed as he started the car and guided it out of the parking lot. He thought she'd gone to sleep until her eyes opened and she asked, "Griff? Who's a jerk?"

Remembering that she'd overheard him muttering in the canteen, he answered candidly. "I am."

"Oh." She closed her eyes again, smiling faintly. "Yeah, sometimes you are."

He couldn't hold back a chuckle. "Why don't you catch a nap. I'll wake you when we get there."

"Mm." She sounded half asleep already. Her voice was just the slightest bit slurred when she spoke again. "Griff?"

"Yeah?"

"I love you anyway."

The car swerved sharply. Bringing it under control, he half turned to her, only to find her sound asleep, her hand tucked under her cheek against the back of the seat, her legs curled under her, hair tumbling around the pale oval of her face. He cleared his throat almost soundlessly and turned to concentrate on his driving. He was in a considerably more cheerful frame of mind when he pulled into a parking space and turned off the engine.

Melinda loved him. Knowing all there was to know about him, agreeing that he could be a jerk at times, disapproving as she was of his career, she loved him anyway.

He must have done something right.

And he'd do whatever he had to do to make sure she didn't stop loving him.

". . . AND I'M SETTING HIM UP on a schedule of weekly visits for the next few months. Oh, and make a note to stock up on soft drinks for his visits."

Finishing her notes for the secretary to type later, Melinda turned off the tape recorder and set it aside, then reached immediately for another file. She'd tried to stay busy, but she'd been aware that thoughts of Griff had hovered in the back of her mind all day.

Composed and professional on the outside, she'd gotten through a staff meeting and several appointments without giving any indication that she was being haunted by questions for which she had no answers. What lay in the future for her and Griff? Would he ever open up to her, ever share his deepest feelings with her? Would he ever learn that he could be himself and still be a success, that it wasn't necessary to adopt a bland facade for the benefit of everyone but her? Had she ruined everything by letting him know that she wasn't willing to play along with his pretenses, that a future with her would include reminders of the past? And, most importantly, how *did* he feel about her? Did he even *want* a future with her?

He'd taken her home from the hospital last night and left her at her door with a kiss, bidding her to sleep well. Granted, the kiss had been tender and lingering, giving no indication that he was annoyed with her or that he wanted to end their relationship. But neither had he said anything about his feelings for her or about the confrontation they'd had before they'd been interrupted by the call from the hospital. He'd never given an answer to her invitation to accompany her to Springfield for Thanksgiving.

Still physically and emotionally drained, Melinda hadn't tried to talk him into staying the night, nor had she pushed him for answers, telling herself they could wait until she was rested. She was already more than half asleep when she'd fallen into bed shortly afterward, having taken time only to change into a sleep shirt and brush her teeth.

Sometime in the middle of the night, she'd sat straight up in bed, wide awake, one hand covering her mouth as she realized that she'd told him she loved him! Though she'd been barely conscious when the words had left her mouth, she quite clearly remembered saying them . . . and then she'd fallen asleep without giving him a chance to reply.

Was that why he'd left so abruptly? Had she scared him off with her ill-timed declaration? If only she hadn't been so tired, so dazed with the events of the evening. If only she'd waited for the right moment to break it to him that she was in love with him. But no. She'd had to blurt it out at the worst possible time, probably ruining everything.

"Why do I *do* things like that?" she demanded of Fred as he walked into her office carrying a newspaper under his arm.

"I give up," he said equably. "Why *do* you do things like that? And what, by the way, did you do in your own inimitable manner?"

"Oh, never mind," she answered with a sigh, waving a hand to dismiss the subject. "It's just too complicated to discuss right now."

"Does it have anything to do with a certain up-and-coming young attorney? One who happens to be involved in a nationally publicized court case at the moment? One who's been seen—and photographed—with the very psychologist who testified against him in his last big case?"

"Fred, what are you—" She stopped abruptly, her eyes widening as she watched him draw the newspaper from under his arm and hold it conspicuously in front of him. "Photograph? What photograph?" she asked apprehensively.

"This photograph. Quite striking, too, I might add."

The River City *Weekly Journal* landed with an ominous plop on the desk in front of her. She picked it up as warily as she might have lifted an ill-tempered pet. She groaned loudly when she spotted the large, all-too-clear photograph on page three—which Fred had made sure was on top when he'd tossed the paper on her desk. She and Griff had been captured sitting very close together at the city council meeting the week before, his mouth close to her ear, his hand familiarly on her arm. She remembered the moment when he'd advised her not to lose her temper with one of the more redneck audience members. The photograph made it appear that he was advising her on even more weighty matters.

What interest did prominent St. Louis attorney Griffin Taylor have in River City politics? the accompanying article asked. Or was his interest a more personal one? The local gossip column went on to identify Melinda and her role in the Nancy Hawlsey trial, commenting on the irony of her dating Griff. It mentioned that she'd recently been spotted as a spectator in the Stanley Schulz trial, after which she had heatedly defended Griff's professional record, despite her admission that she considered Schulz negligent in the fire that had taken six lives.

The column also included speculation that, though he had become known as a very private person who did not encourage publicity, Griffin Taylor was considered a likely candidate for political office in the near future, mentioning several public offices that were rumored to hold interest for him. Perhaps his rather defiant relationship with the outspoken psychologist indicated that there was more to the man than the conservative, intense, no-nonsense image he'd presented during the past couple of years, the writer concluded.

Melinda didn't have to read the byline to know that the columnist was Joe McLeod, the reporter who'd detained her in the courtroom hallway.

Groaning again, she dropped the newspaper and hid her face in her hands. "Great. This is all I need," she muttered, appalled. The timing couldn't have been worse. Griff hadn't let her know whether he wanted a permanent relationship with her, and now it had been publicly announced that they were seeing each other. "What will Wallace Dyson say?" she wondered aloud.

"Maybe he won't see it," Fred suggested encouragingly.

"Oh, sure. And maybe it'll snow in the Sahara Desert tomorrow."

"Come on, it's only a small weekly paper and this meeting happened days ago. Why would Dyson read about it?"

She thought of Doyle Myers, Griff's snidely jealous associate. Someone like that would be all too delighted to make sure Dyson saw the article. "He'll see it," she predicted glumly. "And he won't like it. Poor Griff. Look what I've gotten him into now."

"What *you've* gotten him into?" Fred repeated. "Did you force him to go with you to that meeting, Melinda?"

"Well, no. In fact, I tried to talk him out of it."

"There you go. This is not your fault. Besides, it had to come out eventually that he was seeing you."

"If he continued seeing me," she agreed cautiously.

"As if there were any question of that. It's obvious that the two of you are crazy about each other."

"How would you know. You've never even met Griff."

He leaned over to tap the photo with one blunt finger. "I've got eyes."

Following his lead, she looked at the photograph. Okay, so maybe she was looking at Griff as if he were the only man in the world. And maybe—just maybe— he was looking at her with much the same expression. Maybe it was a trick of the light or something.

She turned her eyes to her friend and for once she wasn't able to hide her fears. "I love him, Fred. I love him more than I ever dreamed it was possible to love someone. And I don't want to cause trouble for him. If this is the kind of thing that's going to happen to him if he keeps seeing me, maybe it would be best if we end it now. He has such a wonderful future ahead of him. I don't want to mess it up for him."

"No, you wouldn't want to do that," he concurred gravely, his tone rather sarcastic. "If you're not careful, you might even make the man happy. We can't have that for a future political candidate, now can we?"

She shoved the paper off her desk. "Something tells me that this is not going to make him happy."

"Why don't you wait and let him tell you how he feels about it before you throw yourself in front of a train for his sake?"

"Fred, stop making jokes. This is serious."

"So am I," he retorted. "You're beating yourself up for no reason. Griff's a grown man. You haven't coerced him into dating you, nor have you trapped him into any kind of commitment. If he wants you, if he loves you— hell, if he has any sense at all—he'll be willing to put up with occasional obnoxious gossip in order to be with you."

"And if this Joe McLeod decides that Griff's interesting enough to investigate further?" she demanded, voicing her gravest concern. "How's he going to break the news that Griff was a rebellious teenager from an unsavory home situation, that he was always getting into trouble with the local authorities and that he went into the Navy to get away from a dead-end situation in Springfield? Will he get his hands on Griff's senior picture from the high school yearbook—the picture with the long hair and earrings and black eyeliner? Don't you know how embarrassing that would be for Griff?"

Fred shrugged, though his expression was not unsympathetic. "Maybe, but it's a part of his past that he'll have to learn to live with. If he's seriously considering public office, he can always use that type of background to his advantage. People admire someone who can make something of himself against all odds, who has risen above the disadvantages to make a success of himself. And, face it, there aren't many people who'd want their high school pictures published. You should see mine. Talk about the quintessential nerd! I even had horn-rimmed glasses and a pocket protector full of pencils and markers!"

Intrigued, she lifted one eyebrow, momentarily distracted. "You're kidding."

"Nope. President of the chess club," he added glumly.

She couldn't help laughing. And then she remembered her problem. "You're doing it again," she accused. "You refuse to admit how serious this is."

"I'm only putting it into perspective. Griff can use this to his advantage, or he can ignore it the way he does his unhappy memories. And someday all those repressed feelings are going to rip him apart."

She sighed. "That's what I told him."

"It's what any good counselor would tell him. And you're good, kid."

She sighed again. "I'm too deeply involved this time. I can't be objective."

"No. That's what's keeping you from realizing that you've done all you can do. You still think you have to protect him—from publicity, from his past, from you, even from himself. But there's nothing else you can do, Melinda. It's up to Griff now."

It's up to Griff now. Hearing Fred say the words made her realize exactly how true they were. She'd made her own feelings quite clear. And now it was up to Griff.

She'd always been so confident that her life was in her hands. Even as a child, she'd known what she wanted, gone after it in her own way. She wasn't accustomed to placing her future in someone else's hands. And yet that was exactly what she'd done with Griff.

She'd survive if he decided their relationship wasn't worth the trouble. She'd even try to understand. But she'd never again know the happiness she'd found in Griff's arms.

11

GRIFF WAS GETTING READY to leave late that afternoon when he was summoned to Dyson's office.

"He sounded furious," Madeline, his secretary, told him with some concern.

After spending a fruitless moment trying to remember anything he might have done to displease his boss, Griff shrugged and stood, reaching for the jacket to his suit. "Oh, well, I guess he'll let me know whatever it is I've done wrong."

Wincing, Madeline nodded. "Want me to hang around for a while?"

He chuckled and patted her plump shoulder. "Go home. I can take it."

"See you tomorrow, Griff. I hope," she added ominously.

He was grinning when he walked out of the office, amused by his secretary's histrionics. Whatever Dyson had to say, it couldn't be that bad, he figured.

It was immediately apparent that Wallace Dyson was every bit as disturbed as Madeline had warned. The older man glared fiercely at Griff, his heavy brows lowered, his mouth set in a thin, straight line. "Have you seen today's *Weekly Journal*, Mr. Taylor?" he asked without preliminary—and without inviting Griff to be seated.

Feeling as if he were in the service, Griff barely restrained himself from standing at military attention. Instead, he kept his posture deceptively relaxed as he considered the question. "No, sir, I haven't. It's not a newspaper that I read very often."

Dyson slapped the paper on his desk, facing Griff. "Perhaps you'd like to look at it now. And then maybe you'd like to explain what the hell you're doing in it."

Inwardly wincing, Griff lifted the paper and studied the photograph on page three. It took him only a couple of minutes to read the accompanying article. The coy, gossipy tone of the column turned his stomach, but he kept his expression bland as he set the paper on the desk. "Obviously some young reporter is hoping for a better job than columnist for a small weekly rag."

Dyson's brow furrowed even more deeply. "That's all you have to say?"

"What would you like me to say, sir? I don't care for this type of irresponsible prattle, but there's nothing blatantly false in the article. I did attend that meeting."

"With that woman."

Griff very deliberately straightened his glasses, holding on to his temper with an effort. He didn't care at all for the way Dyson had referred to Melinda, but he had nothing to gain by expressing his anger at the moment. "With Melinda James," he agreed pointedly.

"You've been seeing her regularly?"

"We've been dating. As I told you once before, Melinda and I knew each other as kids. The Hawlsey case was the first time we'd seen each other in several years, and we've enjoyed spending time together again." He didn't think he owed Dyson explanations, but he needed a momentary diversion to regain his control before responding to any more questions in Dyson's accusatory tone.

"So that's why you've been avoiding my Leslie. That wasn't very gentlemanly of you to lead her on and then drop her that way, Taylor. I expected better of you."

Griff's jaw tightened. "I never led your daughter on, Mr. Dyson. Leslie's a charming woman and I enjoyed her company on the few occasions we were together, but there was never any indication on either side that we had a more serious relationship."

"You've dropped Leslie to date a woman who testified against one of our most influential clients, a man who has been with us for years. What do you think Arthur Dayton will say if he reads that you're dating the woman who played a part in costing him a great deal of money? How do you expect Stanley Schulz to react if he reads that you're on intimate terms with a woman who has publicly announced that she considers him little better than a murderer because he didn't install a sprinkler system in his building, despite the fact there was no legal requirement for him to do so at the time the building was constructed?"

Ignoring the part about Leslie, Griff concentrated on the more valid reasons for Dyson's distress. "I understand your concerns, Mr. Dyson, but our clients will just have to realize that, regardless of what I choose to do on my own time, I represent them to the best of my ability in the courtroom. I think my record speaks for itself. I'm good at what I do. They asked for me because they know that."

Dyson grunted, but Griff knew the other man hadn't taken offense at Griff's quiet statement of his own worth. Dyson had no use for false modesty. Griff also knew that the confrontation wasn't over. Not by a long shot.

"Mr. Taylor, when I hired you, I did not do so blindly. I recognized the potential in you, but I wanted to know exactly what kind of man I was adding to my team—much more than you gave us in your rather sketchy résumé. I had you investigated. I know about your juvenile record, about your less than respectable family history. Still, I've always considered myself a shrewd judge of character and I knew that you had unlimited potential with the proper guidance."

Griff swallowed hard, then managed, "Thank you, sir."

"I'm going to offer you a bit of that guidance now, Taylor. You've got a hell of a future ahead of you. I've spearheaded more than a few successful political careers, as I'm sure you know, and I can do the same for you. State representative, congressman, senator, governor—you name what you want, I can help you get it. We can use your past to your advantage if we're careful—the self-made man angle, folks like that.

"But," he added with a meaningful scowl, "to overcome a background like that, you've got to live an exemplary life. You have to be a model of society, conform to every expectation of a proper public servant. I've always suspected that you were aware of that, and that you had every intention of doing whatever was necessary to get ahead. You haven't given me a moment of doubt in two years."

"Until now," Griff supplied crisply.

Dyson nodded. "Until now. She isn't right for you, Taylor. You need a woman who knows her place as the mate of a man who is destined for power and celebrity. A woman who'll support you in private and public, a woman who'll keep her own opinions to herself if they happen to conflict with yours. Some politicians get away with having outspoken, even eccentric wives. You wouldn't. This woman—well, she's poison for you."

His fingers twitched, but Griff managed to keep his hands from clenching into fists. He couldn't remember ever being this angry, but he was determined that Dyson would not detect his feelings. Not until he was ready to reveal them. "You think I should dump her?"

Dyson looked pained at the blunt phrasing. "I think it would be best if you stop spending so much time with her," he amended. "The gossip will die down if you're seen with other women at your side."

"Leslie, for example?"

Dyson's eyes narrowed, his mouth tightened. "Leslie has been raised to know what's expected of the wife of a prominent man. However, if she doesn't interest you, there are other, equally suitable young women in our social circles."

"Should I consider this 'guidance' to be in the form of an order, Mr. Dyson?"

"Take it any way you like, Mr. Taylor."

"You'll understand if I ask for some time to consider your advice?"

"Of course." Dyson lifted the offensive newspaper between his thumb and forefinger and dropped it in the wastebasket. "We'll consider the matter closed for now.

I can expect to see you at the cocktail party tomorrow evening?''

The firm would be celebrating its twenty-fifth anniversary in business at that party, which would include all of its influential clients, as well as most of the cream of St. Louis society. Invitations to the event had been highly coveted during the past weeks. Griff had known all along that he'd have to attend, though he'd been cravenly putting off the decision of whether to ask Melinda to be there as his date. His chest tightened in disgust at his own cowardice. "I'll be there."

"Good. And, by the way, Leslie had planned to attend with my wife and me. Perhaps you'd like to give her a call this evening? I'm sure she'd rather be escorted by someone closer to her own age."

Griff responded with a noncommittal murmur, choosing not to reveal that his plans had been made moments before. "May I go now, sir? I have a great deal to do this evening."

Eyeing him suspiciously, obviously unable to read anything in Griff's expression, Dyson exhaled in frustration and motioned curtly toward the door. "Fine. Go. But don't forget what I said."

"I won't forget a word, Mr. Dyson," Griff assured him. And then he turned on one heel and left the room, too coldly angry to trust himself to say any more. Dyson would learn soon enough how Griff responded to being told how to live. And to having the woman he loved referred to as "that woman" in a tone that had made him quiver to knock the older man out of his chair.

MELINDA PACED her living room, wondering what had happened to Griff. It was nearly ten o'clock and he hadn't dropped in, hadn't phoned. She'd called his apartment three times and he hadn't answered. He'd always let her know before when he'd be unavailable. She'd gotten into the habit of expecting him to do so. Was he tied up with business or out with someone else? Leslie Dyson, for example.

Had he seen the article? If so, what had he thought? Had it made him realize just how risky his relationship with her would be? Was that why he was avoiding her now?

Just as the questions threatened to turn into a full-scale anxiety attack, the telephone rang. She snatched it before the second ring. "Hello?"

"Hi."

"Griff," she breathed, her fingers loosening in relief as she sagged onto the couch.

"How's Twyla?"

"She's better. I stopped by the hospital on my way home."

"That's good. I forgot to tell you that I was really proud of you last night, Melinda. You're very good at what you do. I don't want you to think that I don't know that, or that I'm unaware of what a valuable service you provide for your clients."

"Why, thank you," she answered, surprised by his words. What had brought *that* on? Was this a gentle preliminary to a breakup? Oh, God, she didn't think she could be professional and detached if he told her he didn't want to see her again. She really thought she might burst into tears—and then go after him with both fists. How dare he break her heart?

Seeming oblivious to her seething emotions, Griff continued to speak rather blandly. "You were wiped out when I left last night. Did you sleep well?"

The carefully polite conversation had her on the verge of screaming, but she managed to answer in the same vein. "Yes, thank you."

"The reason I called is to ask you to a company function tomorrow night," he said, abruptly changing the subject.

"A company function?" she repeated, puzzled.

"Yeah. It's a cocktail party to commemorate the firm's twenty-fifth anniversary. I'd like you to be my date. I'm sorry I waited until so late to ask you, but I wasn't sure you'd be interested. It's going to be pretty dull, I'm afraid."

She had to clear her throat before she could speak. When she did, her voice was still rather husky. "Griff, are you sure you want me to go to this with you?"

His answer was immediate and firm. "I'm absolutely certain."

Her heart thudded in her throat. Did this mean what it sounded like? Was he telling her that he didn't care what other people thought of their relationship? That she was more important to him than anything else? One hand resting on that pounding pulse in her throat, she asked slowly, "Griff, did you happen to see the *Weekly Journal* today?"

"I saw it."

"And?"

"We'll talk about it tomorrow, okay? It's getting kind of late tonight. So, what about the party, Melinda? Will you go with me?"

"If you're sure you want me to."

"I am. And I really hate to ask this, but would you mind meeting me there? I'm going to be tied up until the last minute."

"All right. Where and when?"

He gave her the details. "So I'll see you then?"

"Yes."

"Good. Sleep well, Melinda."

He hung up before she could respond, leaving her to stare in bewilderment at the buzzing receiver in her limp hand. Finally, she placed it in its cradle and stood to slowly walk into her bedroom.

What a strange conversation! So much implied, so much left unsaid.

Griffin Taylor was going to drive her certifiably insane if she wasn't careful, she thought with a perplexed shake of her head.

And then she broke into a smile. He'd asked her to his company party! He wanted her as his date, right in front of Wallace Dyson and Doyle Myers and all his other associates! That had to mean something.

She stood for a long time in her walk-in closet, frowning at the colorful array of garments hanging there. What would she wear? The silver? No, too revealing. The fuchsia? Too loud. The blue? Too outrageously styled. She was determined to show Griff that she could fit in with his peers, that she wouldn't embarrass him. If it meant subduing her individuality for his sake, she'd do it.

Suppressing the uncomfortable feeling that she would be no happier in a narrow mold than Griff had been during the past few years, she concentrated on selecting an outfit. She settled finally on a black dress she found stuffed in the back of the closet, a conservative, formally proper garment she'd never really liked. She'd wear it with neat little gold earrings and a thin gold chain, she decided, though she thought longingly of a splashy faux ruby and emerald set that would really liven up the almost severe dress.

That night she dreamed that she was cast in a 1950s situation comedy. In it, she wore a trim cotton housedress beneath a frilly lace apron, a neat strand of pearls around her throat as she packed Griff's lunch. She handed him his lunch and briefcase and saw him off to work with a kiss at the door. And then she turned on the vacuum cleaner and spent the rest of the day cleaning her floors with a vacant, ecstatic smile, perfectly content with the sacrifice of her own personality for the sake of Griff's success.

As nightmares went, it was one of the worst she'd ever had. She woke in a cold sweat, wishing she could have dreamed of something less disturbing. Like man-eating monsters or a room full of spiders and snakes.

Groaning, she covered her head with her pillow and tried to convince herself that she was really very happy.

BECAUSE SHE HAD a late appointment on Friday afternoon, Melinda didn't have time to go home to change before meeting Griff at the cocktail party at the time he'd designated. She changed at the office, spending half an hour in the restroom working on her hair and makeup. When she was finished, she took a long look at herself in the mirror above the sink.

The dress had long, full sleeves with deep cuffs, a snug bodice with a sedate jewel neckline, a narrow waist emphasized by a wide matching belt, and a mid-calf-length skirt that swirled softly when she moved. She wore black heels and carried a tiny black bag—her only other accessories the small gold earrings and thin gold chain she'd selected the night before. Though she usually preferred bold evening makeup, with particular emphasis on her unusually shaped emerald eyes, she'd been much more conservative in her application this time, choosing subdued colors applied with a light hand. She'd pinned her thick strawberry-blond mane into a prim chignon, mentally crossing her fingers that it would stay up at least until she and Griff left the party.

She looked well enough, she supposed. Quite attractive, actually. She just didn't look like Melinda.

Taking a deep breath, she stepped furtively out of the restroom, hoping she'd be able to escape without encountering either of her partners. No such luck. She almost collided with both of them just as she reached the front door to the clinic.

"Kind of late in the day for a funeral, isn't it, Mel?"

"Don't start with me, Murphy."

"*I* think she looks very nice."

"Thank you, Fred."

"It's not easy to look beautiful when you're in mourning. Whose funeral you going to, Melinda?"

"Dammit, Fred! Not you, too."

Crossing his arms over his turquoise and canary yellow sweater, Murphy subjected Melinda to a lengthy examination. "That outfit needs something," he concluded.

"What?" she answered warily.

"Someone else to wear it. It's just not you, kid. Go home and put on that silver thing you wore to the auction. Or the hot pink you wore at the Handleman party last month. The one that made the butler put on sunglasses to serve you hors d'oeuvres."

"How about that white outfit that's cut up to here and down to there? The one with the big red belt that's the only thing holding it on your body. I like that one," Fred suggested with a teasing leer.

"Look, it's not that kind of party, okay? What I'm wearing will be just fine."

"So it *is* a funeral."

She barely resisted stamping her foot. "It's not a funeral. It's a cocktail party for Griff's firm. To celebrate the twenty-fifth year in business."

The identical looks of concern that creased her partners' faces would have been amusing had she not so fully agreed with them. "You can't start this, Mel," Murphy said gravely. "It won't work."

"You're doing the same thing Griff is—making yourself fit into a mold to please someone else," Fred concurred. "It's a disaster waiting to happen."

She held up both hands, palms out, in a gesture of surrender. "I know. Believe me, I know. And I'm not going to make a practice of this. Really, I'm not," she repeated when both men looked skeptical. "It's just that this is the first time I've gone with him to something like this and I—well, I want to make a good impression. For Griff's sake."

"And when you meet Stanley Schulz?" Fred quizzed. "You going to shake his hand and tell him what an honor it is to meet him? Tell him that reporter was all wrong, that you don't really blame Schulz for the deaths in that fire?"

She lifted her hands to her temples, where a dull ache was beginning to throb in earnest. "I don't know. Okay? I just don't know."

Murphy looped an arm around her shoulders, leaning over to kiss her cheek. "Don't worry about it, honey. It'll work out. When the time comes, you'll know what to do."

"You'll do fine, kid," Fred seconded. "Just keep in mind that you never have to pretend to be anything other than what you are. Melinda James. A damned fine person."

She reached out to include him in the group hug. "You sweet talker, you."

Murphy slapped her heartily on the shoulders. "Go get 'em, Mel."

Amazingly enough, she was smiling when she left, some of her confidence renewed as she looked forward to being with Griff again.

MELINDA HAD EXPECTED to find Griff waiting for her at the entrance to the country club ballroom where the party was being held. He wasn't. She gave her name at the door. The receptionist checked a list, smiled and nodded. "Just go right on in, Ms. James."

Scanning the milling, formally dressed crowd in the ballroom, Melinda hoped to spot Griff. Being taller than average, he shouldn't have been that hard to find. Except that she didn't see him anywhere. Where was he?

Feeling miserably out of place, she accepted a glass of champagne from a courteous waiter and then stood close to a wall, holding the glass in her hands as she watched for Griff, her temper beginning to seethe. Wouldn't he know how uncomfortable this would be for her? Where was he?

"Melinda? I thought that was you. How are you?"

Melinda turned her head to find Leslie Dyson at her side, dressed in a long, shimmery gown of peach silk that was much more flattering than the dress she'd worn the last time Melinda had seen her. "Hello, Leslie. I'm fine, thank you. And you?"

"Very well. Are you here with Griff? I haven't seen him yet this evening."

"Neither have I," Melinda admitted ruefully. "He asked me to meet him here, but I can't find him. Maybe he's playing a practical joke on me," she added with an attempt at a laugh.

Leslie smiled. "Oh, Griff wouldn't do anything like that," she assured her. "He's much too dependable."

Melinda rolled the word around in her head for a moment. Leslie had made "dependable" sound almost synonymous with "boring." It was a close enough association for Melinda, but she hadn't expected Leslie to feel the same way. And, besides, how could any woman ever hint that there was anything dull about Griff?

Unless, of course, he'd been totally different with Leslie than he'd been with Melinda. Maybe Melinda had been the only one privileged to see the real Griff Taylor recently.

"I saw the picture of the two of you in the *Journal*," Leslie confided, stepping closer to Melinda and lowering her voice to a near whisper.

Had *everyone* seen that supposedly obscure little paper? Melinda wondered in exasperation, even as she murmured, "Did you?"

"Yes. You make a nice couple. It was obvious even in that picture that he's crazy about you. I'd suspected as much when I saw you together at the auction."

"Leslie, I—"

"Oh, you don't have to worry about me," Leslie assured her hastily, resting her hand on Melinda's arm. "To be honest, I like Griff well enough, but I'm delighted that he's seeing someone else. Maybe now my father will stop trying to shove us at each other."

"You mean that?" Melinda was genuinely pleased that Leslie seemed to approve of her relationship with Griff. Though Melinda was certain Griff and Leslie would have been a disaster together, she had never wanted Leslie to be hurt.

"Yes, I really do. In fact—" Leslie looked around hastily and lowered her voice even more, so that Melinda had to strain to hear above the party sounds around them. "I've been seeing someone. My father doesn't know about it. He—he wouldn't approve. But I think it's serious. At least it is for me."

"Why wouldn't your father approve?"

"Ross—the man I'm seeing—isn't from the same social circles my family moves in. He's—well, he's the mechanic who works on my car. That's how I met him, when I took the car in for repairs a couple of months ago. I've been sneaking around to see him ever since.

He's really wonderful. It bothers him that I have money and that my family wouldn't approve of him, but I think he really cares for me."

Studying the fresh sparkle in Leslie's formerly impassive eyes, Melinda tried not to let her concern show. "I'm happy for you, Leslie."

She obviously hadn't hidden her feelings as well as she'd hoped. Leslie made a face and then smiled sheepishly. "I know. I can't keep hiding my relationship with him. And I won't for much longer. I just wanted to . . . savor it for a little while before Daddy started trying to interfere."

"Leslie, if you ever need anyone to talk to, give me a call, okay? I've been told I'm a good listener." Melinda smiled. "And I'm not soliciting new business. I'd listen as a friend. No charge."

Leslie returned the smile. "I like you, Melinda. I'm glad Griff found you. Oops, Doyle Myers is standing by Daddy, pointing this way. What do you want to bet the little weasel's telling him who you are? I hate to do this to you, but I think I'll just move on."

"I don't blame you." Melinda sighed, eyeing Dyson's stern expression as he started her way. "See you later, Leslie. And if you see Griff, head him this way, would you? Immediately."

"Good luck."

"Thanks. I may very well need it."

12

LESLIE WAS GONE by the time Dyson reached Melinda's side. "Ms. James, isn't it?"

"Yes, I'm Melinda James. And you must be Mr. Dyson. It's very nice to meet you." Intending to disarm him, she transferred her wineglass to her left hand and extended her right in a friendly gesture.

The handshake was notably brief. "You know my daughter, Ms. James? The two of you seemed quite friendly."

"We've met several times. I like her."

"Mmph." Dyson's mutter was decidedly skeptical. Melinda knew he blamed her for coming between Leslie and Griff and wondered how she could do that to a woman she claimed to like. Lifting her chin, she told herself that she would not allow this man to cause her to lose her temper, to do or say anything that would embarrass Griff. She was well aware that there was quite a bit of surreptitious attention being turned their way.

"You're here with Taylor?"

She nodded. "I'm meeting him here. He must have been detained."

Dyson drew himself to his full height and lowered his heavy brows—a gesture he must have employed whenever he wanted to intimidate. "I'm not going to beat around the bush with you, Ms. James. Griffin Taylor has a brilliant future ahead of him. I'd hate to see anything—or anyone—jeopardize that future."

"So would I, Mr. Dyson," she assured him coolly.

"Then you'll understand when I suggest that you should stop seeing him. Particularly after your imprudent comments to a reporter concerning Griff's clients. Surely you know that behavior such as that can only harm him professionally."

"Mr. Dyson, I—"

Before she could say anything else, a deep, almost lazily amused voice interrupted her. "Hey, yo. Melinda. Did you think I'd stood you up?"

Melinda looked around. Her breath caught in a gasp. "Savage!"

The fascinated spectators were almost as startled by Melinda's unintentional use of Griff's nickname as they were by his appearance. Almost.

Had he dressed like this in the courtroom where they'd been reunited, Melinda would have known him immediately. His short, usually neat hair was sexily disarrayed, brushed back to reveal the golden highlights in its brown depths. Without the glasses he often wore, his chocolate brown eyes, framed in their thick black lashes, were as defiant as Melinda had ever seen them, daring anyone to criticize him. He looked strong and toughly masculine in a worn black leather jacket over a khaki shirt, thin black leather tie and low-slung, rather baggy pleated black slacks. His boots looked as if they'd seen better days.

The silver cross that dangled from his left earlobe was one Melinda recognized—as she did the jacket. So the little wooden plaque hadn't been the only thing he'd saved from his youth, she thought, rather dazed. Where had he kept these things? In a box stashed at the back of a closet, hidden even from himself?

His eyes locked with hers and he winked. She smiled joyously in response, almost giddy with relief. Everything was going to be all right.

"Mr. Taylor!" Dyson barked furiously, drawing Griff's attention. "What is the meaning of this? This firm has a dress code for company functions."

"Yes, sir. And, as you can see, I'm wearing both a jacket and a tie."

"You no longer value your job with Dyson and Associates?" Dyson inquired in cold, unmistakable threat.

"No, Mr. Dyson, I do not," Griff answered unexpectedly, his arms crossed over his chest in a pose of utter self-confidence. "Not if it means that I have to live a lie. Not if it means that my every thought and action will be dictated by you. And not if it means having the woman I love subjected to attacks by my employer or my associates."

Melinda bit her tongue to prevent another gasp of delighted surprise. He loved her. Griff loved her!

"You're the one who threatened me with my past, Mr. Dyson," Griff continued. "You told me that I could turn that past to my advantage—or have it used against me. Well, this is my past, like it or not. My upbringing made me what I am, and it will always be a part of me. It took Melinda to give me the courage to admit that to myself and to you. Melinda was a part of my past, and she is very definitely a part of my future."

Again, he looked at Melinda and his smile told her everything he'd left unsaid because of their audience. Things she knew she'd hear in more detail when they were alone.

She could hardly wait.

"Am I to take this performance as your resignation, Mr. Taylor?" Dyson demanded.

"Take it any way you like, Mr. Dyson," Griff responded, giving the words a twist of meaning that puzzled Melinda. They sounded almost like a quote.

Griff turned his head to scan the room, nodding at a couple of his clients. And then he looked at Dyson, who was too angry to speak at the moment. "As I told you before, sir, I'm good at what I do. Damned good. I like my work, and I don't intend to stop doing it. I can continue to work with you, if you can deal with the knowledge that I will not permit interference in my personal life. Or I can join one of the other firms that have been making overtures to me for the past year. That's up to you."

"If you leave, I'm going with you," a man Melinda didn't know said hastily, stepping out of the crowd. "Dammit, Taylor, we've got a trial starting in two weeks and I want you defending me!"

Realizing that his clients were concerned by the drama unfolding in front of them, Dyson held up both hands in conciliation. "Now, don't anyone overreact. Taylor and I have had a disagreement, but those of you who know me will realize that's not uncommon."

An uncertain titter of amusement rippled through the crowd.

"Why don't we finish this in my office on Monday, Taylor," Dyson suggested with an attempt at a smile for the benefit of his clients.

"That would be fine, sir."

"Mr. Dyson," Melinda said quickly when the older man would have walked away.

He turned back warily. "Yes?"

"I want to apologize for any embarrassment I may have caused your firm or your clients because of remarks I unintentionally made to a reporter recently. I can assure you that will not happen again, whatever my personal opinions of your cases. I would never do anything to deliberately embarrass Griff or his clients, just as I know he would never speak so imprudently about any of the clients of my counseling clinic." She made certain that her voice carried clearly to those standing close enough to overhear, determined that no potential clients would be reluctant to retain Griff because of her.

Dyson hesitated, then thanked her gruffly and turned away to soothe any lingering concerns among his clients. From across the room, Leslie caught Melinda's eye and mouthed a silent cheer, one fist waving in a discreet sign of victory. Melinda thought Leslie looked encouraged by the successful rebellion against her father's domineering ways.

A large, warm hand closed around Melinda's waist. "About this dress," Griff murmured.

She smiled up at him, a bit misty-eyed. "What about it?"

"It's very nice, but—well, it's just not you."

Her smile deepened. "I know. I was thinking about giving it to Meaghan."

"I'll buy you another one to replace it," he promised with a devastatingly crooked grin. "Maybe something in red."

Her fingers entwined with his, linking them together. "We'll talk about it," she replied. "Later."

"No."

"But, Griff, I think it's sexy."

"Sorry. The earring has to go. Do you know how long it took me to put that thing in after twelve years?" he demanded, aggrieved.

"I'm surprised the hole hadn't grown over."

"No such luck."

Propping herself over his chest, she toyed with the silver cross.

"You won't wear it occasionally, just for me?"

His hands made a leisurely path from her bare shoulders down her back to linger at her hips. "No, Melinda. It's history. I only wore it tonight to make a point."

"You certainly did that."

"And besides, you nearly ripped my earlobe off when it caught in your hair a few minutes ago."

"Oh. Sorry. I guess I was too—um—distracted to notice. I usually take my earrings off before engaging in strenuous physical activity."

"Now you tell me. Earlier you asked me to keep it on while we—"

"I told you. I think it's sexy," she broke in with a smile. She leaned to kiss him, her fingers threading into his mussed hair. "You'll keep the leather jacket?" she asked against his lips.

"That can stay," he conceded. "For casual occasions. I still intend to wear my suits to work."

"I can live with that." She kissed him again, then raised her head. "I was so proud of you tonight, Griff." It wasn't the first time she'd told him since they'd left the party.

"You know, it wasn't until Dyson practically ordered me to continue to live a charade that I realized just what a dull clone I'd become during the past two years. I hardly had a thought or an action that wasn't dictated to me by someone else, all because I was afraid to be myself. Afraid that I couldn't measure up on my own terms, certain that I had to imitate those who'd already achieved success to be successful on my own."

"Now you know better. Your clients were ready to follow you wherever you went, earring or no."

"Yeah. Some of them, anyway. How about that?"

"By the way, who was that man who stepped forward in such panic when Dyson asked if you were resigning? The one who said his trial starts in a couple of weeks."

Griff grimaced, then answered warily, "I'm not sure you want to know."

Groaning, she hid her face in his shoulder. "Is this another one of those cases I'm not going to approve of?" she demanded, her voice muffled.

"I'm afraid so. But the man deserves a—"

"Fair trial. I know," she finished, lifting her head to smile at him.

He twisted a lock of her hair around one forefinger, then spoke seriously. "I have changed, Melinda. It hasn't all been pretense. I really do enjoy my work and I have become rather conservative over the years."

"I know that. I love you just the way you are, Griff, establishment leanings and all. I never wanted to change you, I only wanted you to learn to accept yourself. I've changed, too, you know, since we got back together."

"You have? How?"

She gave a little shrug and smiled ruefully. "I guess I've realized that other viewpoints besides my own deserve to be aired, in court and otherwise. That was one reason I wanted to watch you in court with Stanley Schulz. To see whether I could deal with watching you defend someone I didn't approve of." Her smile turned into a wince. "Maybe I'm more like my brother Matt than I've wanted to admit."

Griff feigned dismay, then chuckled. "I think I can live with that. You will marry me, won't you?"

She stiffened, holding herself away from him to stare into his rather smugly smiling face. "You—uh— *marry?*"

"I told you, I'm conservative. Shacking up's just too liberal for a guy like me."

"Stop teasing me. Are you absolutely positive you want to marry me? Shouldn't you take more time to think about it? Maybe you'll decide I really *am* too flaky. Maybe—"

Griff hushed her by placing his hand deliberately over her mouth. "I asked you a question," he reminded her in his stern, dramatic courtroom voice. "Yes or no, Ms. James?"

He lifted his hand only long enough for her to murmur yes, then he replaced it with his mouth.

"You're absolutely sure?" she asked when he finally allowed her to emerge for air.

"I'm absolutely sure," he replied, flipping her onto her back. He then proceeded to demonstrate in graphic detail exactly how serious he was.

Much, much later, it occurred to Melinda as she lay sated and exhausted in Griff's arms that in bed there was much more of the Savage evident than the tame, conservative attorney he claimed to have become.

She fell asleep smiling her satisfaction with that observation.

THERE WAS ONLY ONE MORE hurdle ahead of them. Sitting in the passenger seat of Griff's car, she watched as he grew visibly tense as they drew closer to the Springfield city limits.

"We're going to have a good time, Griff," she promised, laying her left hand—the one sporting the beautiful new diamond ring—on his taut right arm.

He slanted her a look. "So you keep telling me."

She chuckled at the skepticism in his expression. "Really, we will. You liked my family before, right? Well, all of them but Matt."

"Matt's okay."

"See? You even like him now."

"Mm."

"And you surely aren't worried about whether they'll like you."

"I'm not?"

"No, of course not. Merry always liked you. She thought you had a charming smile. She was right, of course."

He gave her one of those smiles then, and it had the predictable effect of melting her spine. "What about the rest of them?"

She tried to remember what they'd been talking about before his smile had emptied her mind. Oh, yes. Her family. "Marsha always kept an open mind about you. You know her, she likes everyone."

"And Meaghan?"

"Meaghan was scared to death of you," she confessed ruefully. "But don't worry about it. Meaghan always was the nervous type."

He shook his head. "I never understood how two girls who looked so identical could be so different in personality. *You* were never afraid of anything. Still aren't."

Her fingers tightened on his arm. "That's not quite true. I was terrified that you and I wouldn't be able to work out our differences. That you'd decide to marry Leslie Dyson, after all."

"Then you were an idiot," he told her equably.

"You always know just the right, sweet thing to say, don't you, darling?"

He grinned and she was relieved to feel the muscles beneath her hand loosen fractionally.

"I love you, Griff."

His arm relaxed even more. "I love you, too."

"Feeling less nervous now about Thanksgiving with the James clan?"

"Why should I be nervous? I'm about to submit myself to inspection by your two older sisters and their husbands, your brother and his wife, your twin—who thinks I'm a closet sociopath—and her husband, not to mention who knows how many nieces and nephews."

"Seven."

"Thank you. They're all going to be deciding whether I'm a suitable mate for the last single James sister, the youngest and most trouble-prone member of the family. I won't even be able to sleep with you during the three-day ordeal because Meaghan thinks it sets a bad example to the children for unmarried couples to share a bedroom. Yes, I'm really looking forward to it."

Smiling at his melodramatics, Melinda leaned across the console to kiss his cheek. "You'll do fine. You're the hotshot attorney, remember? Just think of them as a jury and use that devastating charm of yours to have them all eating out of your hand. You're very good at that."

"You're good at your work, too. Don't think I'm not aware of what you've been doing."

"And just what have I been doing?"

"Trying to give me something to worry about besides my feelings about returning to Springfield."

"Did it work?"

His eyes focused on a sign that welcomed them to Springfield. "Yeah. For a while."

They rode in silence for the next few minutes. And then Griff made a turn that Melinda hadn't been expecting. "You don't have to do this Griff."

"Yes," he said, keeping his eyes on the road ahead. "I do."

Maybe he was right, she decided, settling into her seat. Maybe this was something he had to do.

The neighborhood was an older one. The frame houses were small and generally run down. Faded paint, broken shutters, peeling wood—signs of poverty relentlessly exposed in the bright afternoon sun. Here and there an attempt had been made to refurbish. A fresh coat of paint over warped, split siding. Lace curtains peeking through a cracked window. Evergreen bushes trying to resemble landscaping.

Griff pulled the car to the curb, staring without expression at one house in particular. It had once been white, the shutters bright blue. Those colors had long since faded. The lawn was neater than it had been twelve years earlier, though the sparse grass was winter brown and the single tree in the front yard nude except for a few clinging brown leaves. A well-used tricycle sat beneath the tree. A small boy of perhaps four sat beside the tricycle, playing with a fleet of inexpensive plastic vehicles. Parked in the driveway was an aging pickup truck with a dented left fender. Watching Griff closely, Melinda wondered if he was picturing his old black Mustang parked in front of that house.

And then the front door opened. Dressed in a blue uniform shirt over faded, somewhat grubby work pants, a man stepped onto the narrow porch, his unstyled hair partially hidden beneath a battered cap, his face shadowed by its brim.

Griff stiffened and Melinda knew he was remembering his father, who'd probably dressed much the same way for the low-paying, blue-collar jobs he'd found and then lost because of his drinking. She covered Griff's white-knuckled hand with her own, wishing she could help him with the demons he must exorcise on his own.

The man looked across the street and frowned at the incongruously expensive car sitting motionless at the curb. He then turned toward the boy playing beneath the tree, motioning for him to come inside. Obediently, the child dropped his toys and hurried on chubby legs toward the house. Reaching the porch, he grinned and launched himself into his father's arms. The man smiled, settled the boy with familiar ease on one hip and ruffled his sandy hair. And then, with one last suspicious look at Griff's car, he turned and entered the house, closing the door behind them.

"Do you know what I would have given to have my father smile at me like that?" Griff murmured, his voice sounding very far away.

"Yes," Melinda answered without hesitation. "I know."

He sighed and turned to her, away from the house and its memories. "I guess you'd have given just as much to have kept your own folks a few years longer."

"I'd have given anything," she replied, her throat tight. "But there was nothing I could do to change what happened to them."

"And nothing I could have done to make my family an ideal, happy one," he finished.

"No." She cupped her hand around his hard cheek. "I'm sorry, Griff. Sorry that you were so unhappy, that the memories still hurt you."

"Not all the memories hurt." He caught her hand and kissed it. "You were the one good thing in my life here. I've never even thanked you for being my friend then."

"It wasn't necessary."

"Yes, it is." He leaned over to kiss her unsteady lips. "Thank you, Melinda. For being my friend then—and now."

Blinking back tears, she managed a smile. "We'd better move on or that man will have the police after us. I think he suspects we're child snatchers at the least."

His smile somewhat strained, Griff started the engine. "That's all I need—another run-in with the Springfield cops."

Fifteen minutes later they stood at the front door of a large, beautiful home in an exclusive neighborhood on the other side of town. From inside, they could hear the muted sounds of conversation and laughter, children playing, a baby crying. The sounds of family.

"Ready?" Melinda asked Griff, her hand clutched tightly in his.

He made a production of squaring his shoulders and checking his clothing—a gray sweater over a white shirt and navy slacks. Melinda had failed to convince him to wear the earring. "I'm as ready as I'm going to get." And then he gave a short laugh. "Damn," he murmured, "I'd almost forgotten."

"Forgotten what?"

He looked into the distance, almost as if he were looking into the past. "Remember the night I told you I was leaving Springfield?"

She shuddered. "Of course I remember. It was the most traumatic experience of my whole adolescence. I cried into Merry's shoulder for hours, convinced that you were leaving because of me."

"Well, I was, but not for the reasons you probably thought. Anyway, I ran into Merry's husband, Grant, after dropping you off that night. Of course, he wasn't her husband then. As I remember, he was almost as frustrated that evening as I was. We probably both went home to cold showers."

Tapping her foot impatiently, she demanded, "So what did you almost forget?"

Smiling at her rampant curiosity, he squeezed her hand. "I warned Grant then that I'd be back for you someday. That was before I made the big decision never to return and locked your memory away with all the others."

"Before you got stupid, you mean," she teased, earning a laugh and a playful slap on the bottom for her impudence.

Giggling, she smoothed her brightly colored outfit and reached for the doorbell. Her fingers hesitated before pressing the button. "One more thing, Griff."

He groaned. "What now?"

"If *our* daughter should ever bring home a young man with shoulder-length hair and ragged clothes and earrings—"

"I'll lock her in her room."

She grimaced. "Just keep an open mind, okay? He could be a truly wonderful person."

"We'll talk about it," he said firmly. "When and if the occasion arises. Ring the bell, Melinda."

She shook her head. "Why do I suspect that my Savage has grown into a man an awfully lot like my brother?" she muttered.

He grinned—that full, loving, unshadowed smile that she adored. "Call it just retribution," he advised, and the wicked glint in his warm brown eyes wasn't at all predictable or conservative.

Maybe the Savage had never been fully tamed, after all, Melinda thought contentedly. And then she rang the doorbell.

HARLEQUIN
American Romance®

THE ROMANCE THAT STARTED IT ALL!

For Diane Bauer and Nick Granatelli, the walk down the aisle
was a rocky road....

Don't miss the romantic prequel to WITH THIS RING—

I THEE WED
BY ANNE McALLISTER

Harlequin American Romance #387

Let Anne McAllister take you to Cambridge, Massachusetts, to
the night when an innocent blind date brought a reluctant Diane
Bauer and Nick Granatelli together. For Diane, a smoldering
attraction like theirs had only one fate, one future—marriage.
The hard part, she learned, was convincing her intended....

Watch for Anne McAllister's I THEE WED, available *now* from
Harlequin American Romance.

ITW

Coming in March from

HARLEQUIN®

LaVyrle Spencer's unforgettable story of a
love that wouldn't die.

LAVYRLE
SPENCER

SWEET MEMORIES

She was as innocent as she was unsure... until a very special
man dared to unleash the butterfly wrapped in her cocoon and
open Teresa's eyes and heart to love.

SWEET MEMORIES is a love story to savor that will make you
laugh—and cry—as it brings warmth and magic into your
heart.

"Spencer's characters take on the richness of friends, relatives
and acquaintances."
                                        —*Rocky Mountain News*

COMING IN 1991 FROM
HARLEQUIN SUPERROMANCE:

Three abandoned orphans,
one missing heiress!

Dying millionaire Owen Byrnside receives an
anonymous letter informing him that twenty-six years
ago, his son, Christopher, fathered a daughter. The
infant was abandoned at a foundling home that
subsequently burned to the ground, destroying all
records. Three young women could be Owen's long-
lost granddaughter, and Owen is determined to track
down each of them! Read their stories in

#434 HIGH STAKES (available January 1991)
#438 DARK WATERS (available February 1991)
#442 BRIGHT SECRETS (available March 1991)

Three exciting stories of intrigue and romance by
veteran Superromance author Jane Silverwood.

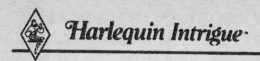

Harlequin Intrigue

A SPAULDING & DARIEN MYSTERY

Make a date with Jenny Spaulding and Peter Darien when this engaging pair of amateur sleuths returns to solve their third puzzling mystery in Intrigue #171, ALL FALL DOWN (October 1991).

If you missed the first two books in this four-book A SPAULDING AND DARIEN MYSTERY series, #147, BUTTON, BUTTON, or #159, DOUBLE DARE, and would like to order them, send your name, address, zip or postal code along with a check or money order for $2.50 for book #147 or $3.25 for book #159, plus 75¢ postage and handling ($1.00 in Canada) for each book ordered, payable to Harlequin Reader Service, to:

In the U.S.
3010 Walden Ave.
P.O. Box 1325
Buffalo, NY 14269-1325

In Canada
P.O. Box 609
Fort Erie, Ontario
L2A 5X3

Please specify book title(s) with your order.
Canadian residents add applicable federal and provincial taxes.